THE FREE-GRAZE WAR

THE FREE-GRAZE WAR

Lauran Paine

Chivers Press • Thorndike Press
Bath, England   Waterville, Maine USA

This Large Print edition is published by Chivers Press, England, and by Thorndike Press, USA.

Published in 2003 in the U.K. by arrangement with the author c/o Golden West Literary Agency.

Published in 2003 in the U.S. by arrangement with Golden West Literary Agency.

U.K. Hardcover   ISBN 0–7540–8847–2 (Chivers Large Print)
U.K. Softcover   ISBN 0–7540–8848–0 (Camden Large Print)
U.S. Softcover   ISBN 0–7862–4836–X (Nightingale Series Edition)

The text of this Large Print edition is unabridged.
Other aspects of the book may vary from the original edition.

Set in 16 pt. New Times Roman.

Printed in Great Britain on acid-free paper.

British Library Cataloguing in Publication Data available

Library of Congress Cataloging-in-Publication Data

Paine, Lauran.
    The free-graze war / Lauran Paine.
       p. cm.
    ISBN 0–7862–4836–X (lg. print : sc : alk. paper)
    1. Ranch life—Fiction. 2. Large type books. I. Title.
    PS3566.A34 F69 2003
    813'.54—dc21
                                  2002073215

CHAPTER ONE

The canyon walls stood high and narrow where they passed through. Out a little ways was the river, at low ebb now because this was late summer. In the canyon strangling dust rose in powder-fine layers to burn the eyes and scald the throat. Thirty-two hundred head of free-graze cattle left that dun-brown banner standing straight up against a faded sky.

At night they camped any handy place but always near the river. The browse was sun-cured and crackling dry but it would sustain young beef and they had long since culled out the gummer cows. As late summertime drives went this one was not progressing badly. Especially in new country. None of the free-graze men had ever been to the Devil's Punch Bowl before, and there were crises almost every day and unforeseen obstacles. Still, they kept seven men scouting on ahead and this eliminated a lot of trail-trouble.

Now and then they came upon Navajos in the creek-willows who would rise up and peer out at the plodding cattle and the nut-brown, lean men who rode with them. But Navajos were a tractable people; they'd rustle a critter now and then if they could, even run off a few horses in the night, given half a chance. But these were not ordinary cowboys, these were free-graze men, which meant they were always on the lookout against strangers, red-skinned or white-skinned. Their environment had formed and sustained them; it was not now and never had been an easy environment.

Free-graze men roamed the West nomad-like. They owned no land and wanted to own none. They drifted herds of cattle and horses on to the public lands, usually in the midst of herds belonging to established cowmen, and they were considered the parasites of the cow country because they habitually over-grazed the land and when it was no longer capable of sustaining their big herds, they moved on to better grass leaving the established cattlemen with thousands of acres of useless, fallow earth, devoid of grass and haunted by the dust-devils of a dead countryside.

Free-graze men spent money only for cattle; they spent none on buildings, on water development, on range improvement. They made money every year, so they were not like other nomads; like Indians for instance or gum-boot settlers who grubbed out a bare living. They were seldom poor men.

They were ordinarily fierce men; they had to be. Established ranchers dreaded a free-graze invasion of their public domain more than they had feared marauding Indians in years past, or even the coming of homesteaders. The Indians had been systematically hunted down and exterminated.

Homesteaders foolish enough to believe a hundred and sixty acres of waterless land would support a man and his family, had only to be waited-out. A year, two years, was about all it took, then the wasted man loaded his brood into a rickety wagon and departed, the land reverted to public domain and the established cowmen saw his spring calves turn greasy fat again among the ruins of empty shacks where sagging gates endlessly squeaked in the total hush of the big country.

But the fear of free-grazers was a solid thing; they came and then moved on leaving in their wake a desolate world. They had down the years bankrupted many a powerful cattle baron by their systematic ruination. But the boot had not always been exclusively on the one foot; free-grazers lay under a scant two feet of summer-hard ground from the Missouri to the Sacramento, sent down to their graves by opposing guns and lynch-ropes, for in the eyes of all established, land-owning cattlemen they were called pariahs and worse.

So, their environment made them fierce. They seldom rode easy; by the very nature of their calling they had to be hair-triggered men who slept always with one eye open. They had large herds and money, good horses and strong wagons, all the requisites for successful operating, but they were neither respected nor liked. To kill a free-graze man was about equal to killing a varmint among the established cowtowns. The trouble was, though, that being despised and feared as they knew themselves to be, free-graze men rarely went anywhere alone, and a brace of them or a band of them was nothing to take lightly; the ones who bore scars from ten dozen battles with the established cowmen, were without any question at all some of the toughest, wiliest, deadliest gunfighters between the Purgatory and the Canadian.

The ranchers had no warning, usually; one day their herds grazed peacefully upon the public lands as they always had; the next day cowboys out salting would encounter strange brands on wicked-horned cattle. It would gradually dawn upon the established cattlemen that free-grazers were amongst them.

So it was at the Devil's Punch Bowl, a huge mountain-locked valley where grass stood stirrup-high and the turgid San Juan ran its crooked, muddy course. One day only occasional bands of Navajos saw the men pass by with their slab-sided Longhorns. The next day they were through the canyons into the valley, their hungry herds fanning out, their wagon-camp established with a texas beside each wagon—peeled saplings stuck into earth, big, soiled widths of canvas stretched overhead—and the rope corrals set up, prepared to stay in the Devil's Punch Bowl until snow flew or grass gave out, whichever came first.

Billy Curtin saw their breakfast fires first from a top-out southward where he rode up to have a casual look at the Graeme herds. He was sure it would be those perennial nuisance, the Navajos, so he paid them no heed until it occurred to him there was quite a bit of smoke, as though perhaps a big band of redskins was camping in the valley. He rolled his brows together at this prospect, thinking that any big come-together of Indians meant someone's herd was sure to come up shy a few fat critters. Billy Curtin rode down off the rimrocks into the Punch Bowl, swung northward keeping to the weak shade along the valley's east side—and came upon a mounted white man athwart his path who had very plainly been sitting there in half-light, half-shadow, watching Billy for some time.

The stranger was a sinewy, leathery man with dead-level blue eyes, a thin slit for a mouth, and a rangy, long-limbed body. He wore a rubber-butted Colt .44 lashed to his right leg and there was a Winchester carbine in a saddle-boot under his right rosadero. He was smoking a brown-paper cigarette, had his hat tipped up over his eyes, and sat easy in his saddle watching Billy come to a quick halt at sight of him. Then he solemnly nodded without saying a word and left it all up to Billy.

The initial reaction for Billy Curtin was to consider that grave stranger a rangerider looking for strays. He didn't work for Jethro

5

Graeme, Billy knew, because of Jethro's seven cowboys Billy had been longest in old man Graeme's employ, first as cook's devil on roundups, then as remuda hostler, and finally, when he'd turned full-grown, as rangerider.

Billy's second reaction was to consider the stranger an outlaw; there were plenty of owl-hoot riders in this back country lying quiet from the law. Then Billy made his final assessment—helped to it by the unmistakable aroma of frying bacon, boiling greens and coffee, things Indians did not eat and outlaws rarely had with them. With this final conclusion, Billy's heart sank and his stomach filled with lead. He swung his head, saw the strange brand on nearby cattle, and swung it back again.

'Mister; you just passin' through?' he asked that silent, motionless man with the dead cigarette drooping from his lipless mouth, hoping with his whole heart this was so—and instinctively knowing it was not so.

'Not exactly,' drawled the rawboned older man. 'We was sort of figurin' to stay a spell.' His unwavering regard of Billy was neither friendly nor unfriendly; he was still waiting for the wind of this unexpected encounter to blow one way or another.

'Are those cattle with the pothook brand yours?'

The stranger spat out his cigarette, considered the closest critters and gravely nodded. 'Some are,' he said, 'an' some aren't. We got two bands with us. When the pothook's branded on the left side, they belong to Buck Handley. When it's on the right side they belong to me.' The stranger looked over at Billy again. 'I'm called Hoyt McElroy.'

Billy had his answer now. These were free-graze men, bane of the sprawling public lands, spoilers of everything they touched. He strained far ahead where that punk-wood smoke was rising straight up in the still morning air. There were four wagons up there. There were the slow-moving shapes of men beneath each texas. Saddled horses were dragging reins as they grazed near the wagons. Billy tried to count the men but could never be sure which ones he'd counted before because they constantly moved.

Hoyt McElroy saw this and quietly said, 'Quite a bunch o' us, sonny. Twenty men all told. Now tell me—who owns them JG critters yonder?'

'Jethro Graeme,' answered Billy, beginning to burn with the excitement of his discovery that free-grazers were in the Punch Bowl, which had been JG open-range since decades before his time. 'The JG lies south-easterly beyond the valley about four miles.'

'An' this Jethro Graeme,' drawled McElroy. 'He's got other riders besides you, boy?'

'Six more.'

7

'I see. An' now—one last thing, then I'll invite you over to the wagons to set with the boys an' eat up a little. This here Mister Graeme—I see in your face, boy, that you don't figure he's goin' to take kindly to havin' other fellers runnin' a few head in this here valley with his critters.'

'A few head,' exclaimed Billy, looking far out and drawing up stiffly in his saddle. 'Mister; by my guess I'd say you fellers brought in close to three thousand head.'

'By golly,' said McElroy admiringly, 'that's plumb close, boy. Plumb close. Yes; we got a mite over three thousand head. Now tell me— your Mister Graeme—he won't like that?'

'For a fact he won't,' stated Billy, lifting his reins.

'Well hell,' said McElroy mildly, 'no call to ride off. Come set a spell with us fellers. We'd like to learn a little about this here country, for y'see we're plumb strangers hereabouts, comin' on from West Texas like we done.'

Billy, soothed a little by McElroy's deceptive mildness, shook his head and boldly said: 'Mister; I'll give you some advice, for what it's worth. Round up them pothook critters and get out of the Devil's Punch Bowl quick.'

'Why?' asked McElroy in the same mild tone, his pale eyes steady, his bronzed face expressionless.

'Mister Graeme's goin' to chew nails an' spit

8

rust when he hears you're up in here.'

'Well now, boy—what'd you say your name was?'

'Billy. Billy Curtin.'

'Well now, Billy—hell—this here is open range. Public domain. National land. Mister Graeme's got no right an' legal title to it. So we got as much right in here as he has. Billy; that's the law. Now maybe you didn't know that, but I'll bet you a pretty Mister Graeme knows it. For a fact, Billy, that's the law. Open range is free-graze; anyone can use it.'

Billy sat mute for half a minute, then he slowly turned his horse and slowly rode back the way he had come. He stopped once, several hundred yards onward, and looked back. Hoyt McElroy was watching him. Hoyt hadn't moved at all.

CHAPTER TWO

Buck Handley was out with the cattle the day after Hoyt McElroy met Billy Curtin. Buck had heard from Hoyt about that meeting, so had their riders in the free-graze camp. Each man among them knew there would shortly be another meeting because the sequence never varied wherever free-graze men went with their homeless herds.

Buck was ten years younger than McElroy.

He was a loose-moving man with smoke-grey eyes half-hidden behind the perpetual squint of a man accustomed to looking out at vast distances. Summertime had burnt its layers of bronze smoothly over Buck Handley's face. His features were even and good to look upon and his build was flat-boned and angularly heavy, the shape of a man who made his living by saddle and rope. In appearance he was a capable man, a confident man, and a dangerous man. Yet there were things moving in the depths of his glance that hinted he might also be a lonely man with private memories and private longings.

He was up along an easterly trail seeing how far the pothook cattle had drifted, assessing the size, the richness, and the seclusion of the Devil's Punch Bowl, when a little rattle of stones on around the trail's immediate curving told him that he was not alone. It was early morning with a coolness to the air; sounds travelled far in this thin, high-country air. Buck stepped off the far side of his animal and waited. Whoever was approaching would not be, he was sure, an assassin sent out by JG; he was making too much noise for that.

The wait was brief. Horse and rider came on around the sidehill. Clearly the rider was doing the same thing Handley had been engaged in, looking outward and downward, because no move was made to check the horse until, with the animal slowing of its volition, that rider's head whipped forward, saw Buck leaning there across his saddle-seat, and jerked the reins up and back. There was pure astonishment upon the stranger's face; evidently there had been no thought given to an encounter up along this little-used trail.

Handley got a shock too, though; the rider was not a cowboy at all; it was a girl, and all the urges of a lonely man moved in him at sight of her. She was still young although no longer in her teens, with ebon hair and a full roundness to her upper body that sang over the separating distance to him. Her heavy lips lay closed with a centre fullness and her eyes were wilful, direct and coolly challenging.

She sat there without taking her eyes off Buck. She seemed to be challenging him to break the hauteur of her composed and beautiful face. She seemed also to know she was desirable in his hungry stare. Her poise said as much as she sat there wordlessly watching him, waiting for him to say something. When he didn't, when he continued to endlessly lean there studying her with his quiet, tough look and his easy although careful stance, a break of curious interest flashed in her downward gaze at him.

'Are you one of the free-graze men?' she asked, and he nodded still without moving or speaking. 'Is it true there are twenty men in your camp and that you've brought three thousand cattle to the Devil's Punch Bowl?'

'If,' replied Buck, 'this big mountain-locked valley is called the Devil's Punch Bowl, why then I reckon it's true enough.'

The girl sat on, considering Buck for a silent moment, before she said, 'I suppose it's pointless to ask how long you expect to remain here with your cattle.'

'No'm, not pointless. We figure to stay as long as there's feed.'

Buck straightened up off his saddle. He looked around and downward so that the handsome girl could see his profile, see how it was with a man drawn inward by those solemn thoughts which ride close to a man much alone. Then he looked back at her.

'My name is Buck Handley,' he said, and waited.

'I am Kate Graeme.'

He viewed her with a greater interest after this, thinking she had the arrogance which oftentimes went with wealth and power. Thinking too, that this was the kind of a woman who could pull a man to her against his will, for she was everything a beautiful woman should be—and more. She was strong-willed and durable, resourceful and not given to ready compromises. She could melt a man or she could freeze him solid with a stare.

'One of our riders was over here yesterday, Mister Handley. He met a man named McElroy. A free-graze man.'

'My pardner, Miss Graeme. Hoyt McElroy.'

12

'Mister McElroy made quite a point of telling our JG rider what the law was, regarding public domain lands and grazing rights. This didn't go down well with my father or our riders.'

Buck met the steady onset of those green eyes. He silently brought forth a little tobacco sack, manufactured a cigarette, lit up and dragged strong smoke in and blew it out again. He met that pushing glance and said, 'It's the same story, always,' and stopped speaking.

'There has been justification, Mister Handley. In fact, there has always been justification.'

He smoked on, looking out over the valley again, his gaze sombre, his thoughts solid and forceful. 'What good does it do to talk?' he asked her. 'Your mind's made up.' He swung back towards her again and concluded what he had to say in the softest voice. 'Twenty of us, Miss Graeme. Hoyt an' me and eighteen hired riders. Look out over that valley; there's enough graze down there for twice the number of cattle grazing it. But you say there's always been justification for the way you folks feel about free-grazers; then what's the point in talking. Your mind's made up.'

Kate Graeme gave him a prolonged study. He seemed to interest her more than antagonise her, and this was something Buck Handley was unaccustomed to from her kind. He dropped the cigarette, ground it underfoot

13

and toed in to step up over leather. Their eyes now met on an equal level.

'There is a kind of stigma that goes with free-graze men,' he told her, 'and folks just automatically classify all free-grazers in the same category. You're doing that right now. Before you rode over here, before we met, you had your mind all nicely made up.' He shortened his reins preparatory to moving off. 'I can't make you think different, ma'm, and I'm not sure I even want to try that, so you go do what you have to do.'

He nodded and started off. She let him get fifty feet along before she said: 'The proof is down there; three thousand of your pothook cattle where always before JG has run only our animals.'

He halted. 'A mighty big valley, ma'm. Like I said, it could handle twice as many critters.'

'But you being here shortens the length of time JG can keep its herds in here. Do you deny that?'

'No, ma'm, I don't deny that.' Buck settled in his saddle, he stared back at her. 'But this is a threadbare argument; I've heard it in five states and two territories an' it always comes out the same. If your JG outfit values this valley so much, why hasn't it filed on the land, gotten deed to it; why did your pappy let it remain public domain?'

Here is where the argument between free-grazers and established cowmen always broke

14

down. There were answers, of course, but not very sound ones. Kate Graeme however offered none of those customary answers; she sat there looking steadily at Buck Handley, and when he thought she was not going to speak, she said, 'Why don't you file on it?' And by answering a question with another question she threw it all back at him, because his answers could not be very sound on this score either.

He made a little faint smile at her. 'You know,' he quietly told her, 'I wouldn't want to get into a real argument with you.'

'You never will if you move on.'

'That's too high a price to pay just for losing an argument, ma'm.'

'Too high a price to pay to save a life, perhaps—your own, Mister Handley?'

His little smile lingered. 'It seldom varies, this kind of meeting. First, we come together; second, we talk a little—get the feel of one another; third; the threat. But usually it's two men, or ten men or fifty men. I never had it happen with a girl before, Miss Graeme.'

'But you've had it happen.'

'Yes'm.'

'Then you know what follows the threat.'

He didn't reply. He searched the beautiful girl's face for a sign of change, for some show of the hardening against him her words implied. It was not there; she was without any particular expression except that same one

15

she'd had earlier; that look of interest.

'JG has seven riders, ma'm. Your cowboy told Hoyt that yesterday. Like I said—we have twenty. Yes'm; I know what follows the threat.'

'Don't be fooled by what Billy told your pardner. JG has seven steady riders, yes, but JG can hire three times as many if it has to. Ten times as many, Mister Handley, and I think my father will do that, too, if he is forced to.

'We're not forcing anyone to do anything, ma'm. All we want is to be left alone.'

'While you settle on JG range.'

Buck regarded her calmly. 'You see how it goes? We're back to that again. It's *not* JG's range, it's public domain. We have a right here too, the same as JG. Sure, you folks used it first and have been here longest—but all that proves is that someone is shortsighted, because you've had years to file on the Devil's Punch Bowl—to get legal title to it—and you've never done it.' He paused, watching her eyes blaze out at him with the first smoke of anger she'd thus far shown, and he softened his tone, gentled it towards her.

'I don't want to fight you. I don't want trouble with your pappy's JG outfit. We're not over-grazing, look for yourself. But we've a right to try an' make a living. If JG interferes with that—why then I expect we'll have to fight back. Listen ma'm; don't judge all free-graze men the same. They aren't all the same any

16

more than all established cowmen are the same.'

'Tell all this to my father,' Kate said. 'He's on his way over here.' She turned her horse and rode only a little distance before that curving mountainside cut her off from Handley's view.

He watched as long as she remained in his sight, then sat on for a while thoughtfully motionless. Afterwards, he pressed on downward towards the valley floor, struck it where shale-rock clattered beneath his horse, and loped northward as far as the wagon-camp.

The sun was nearly overhead but shade lay around the wagons, under each texas, and around where the men worked at the little chores, the harness mending, rein-splicing, the horse shoeing and water hauling, which ordinarily filled daylight-hours at cow camps.

Buck stepped down, tossed his reins to a saddle-warped, grizzled and leather older man, sought out Hoyt McElroy and strode across to him to say that Jethro Graeme was coming. Hoyt, in his habitual manner, turned this carefully over in his mind before commenting upon it, then spoke with the Texas drawl and minimising words which so characterised him.

'Well now; one thing you can say about this JG outfit: They don't let no grass grow under their feet, do they?' He relaxed letting both long arms hang loose, and he slowly turned, slowly ran a rummaging look far out down the valley, then grew very still where dust hung motionless like forest-fire-smoke far southward at that break in the rampart-mountains through which young Billy Curtin had ridden the day before. 'No, sir, they sure don't let no grass grow under 'em, Buckley. Yonder they come sure as God made green apples.'

As Buck looked, Hoyt drifted his drawling voice out over the lazily occupied riders. 'Boys; riders comin' on from the south. Four, five o' you take your guns and ride west; few more o' you do the same an' ride east. The balance o' you just sort of fan out around here an' stand easy. We don't want no trouble an' if we're all spread out and ready for it, why I don't expect there'll be any.'

For a time Buck and Hoyt stood watching that lifting dust in strong silence, while around them their men broke up going one way or another. When only the cook and two or three of the riders still remained at the camp Hoyt looked around, satisfied himself that things were as he wished them, then drawled to Buck Handley that since they'd left the last settlement behind two days earlier, there couldn't be much law in the countryside roundabout. Hoyt let this lie for a moment as he watched mounted-shapes materialise southward.

'So now I'm wonderin',' he said, 'just how

18

much strength this JG outfit has. I mean; are there other established ranches 'round here that'd side with JG against us, if JG was to take a notion to be o'nery.'

'There'll probably be other ranches,' opined Buck. 'There usually are.' He paused, keeping his southward vigil. 'Hoyt; it looks to me like he's got his full crew along.'

'Naturally,' answered McElroy. 'You wouldn't expect no established cowman t'come along with his back bowed an' not bring no extra guns along.'

Buck swung his smoky glance to McElroy. 'It's always the same, isn't it?' he remarked.

Hoyt owlishly nodded, his faded gaze holding hard on the approaching riders. 'Pretty near always. The thing that sort o' sticks in a feller's craw is how high an' mighty these established cowmen act. Like we're scum an' they're a bunch of extra respectable upholders o' everythin' that's right and decent. You know, Buck; someday I'm going to lay into one o' these fellers with all I got.'

'Not today, Hoyt. Not unless this Jethro Graeme pushes for trouble.'

That pattern of dust continued forward but the valley was long so it took some time for the horsemen to be thoroughly recognisable as men. By that time every free-graze man was in place, watching and ready.

A half mile out the bunched-up horsemen slowed. Their own suffocating dust rolled up

19

over them where they plodded along on sweaty horses, staring ahead at the free-graze camp and wagons near the river. When they were close enough, Handley could see that not a word was being spoken among them. He also saw that the older man leading them was thick-shouldered, grey as a badger and with a square-jawed face that was now set in a rock-like way.

'That'n on the young grey'll be Jethro hisself,' muttered Hoyt. 'Looks real friendly—'bout like a bitchwolf at whelpin' time.'

Behind Graeme rode an arrow-straight, dark and solid man who possessed a high-bridged, hawkish nose, and oily black eyes to match. This man carried a shotgun as well as a belt-gun, and a Winchester under his leg.

CHAPTER THREE

Jethro Graeme was, at sixty-five, one of those men to whom success and power had come late in life. He was a direct, taciturn, and forceful man. There were very few shades of grey in life for him; he never confused wrong with right or good with bad.

He was a physically solid man with a thick head of silvery hair. His eyes were a paler hue of the same greeny colour as his daughter's eyes, and while he had been a widower for nearly twelve years, he remained careful of his appearance and his looks. Now, as he reined down the horse under him and put both hands upon the saddlehorn while he gazed steadily ahead at the free-graze wagon-camp with its few visible, unmoving men, he said from the corner of his mouth to the hawk-faced swarthy man slightly to one side of him, 'King; Billy was right as rain. They're free-grazers if I ever saw any.'

And King Lewis, JG's rangeboss, said back to Jethro Graeme, 'Look out a ways; there's a lot of 'em an' they've had time to make a loose sort of surround. We're smack-dab in the middle of it.'

Jethro looked, saw those distant, still figures, returned his gaze forward where two lean men were coming forward away from the wagons, and handed King Lewis his reins.

'It's all right, King. We're only here to talk anyway.'

Jethro got down and waited until Buck Handley and Hoyt McElroy came up. When they nodded Jethro nodded back; there, though, his courtesy ended.

'Boys,' he said to Buck and Hoyt, 'you're trespassing. Never mind tellin' me your rights. You already told my rider yesterday what was legal. Now I'm here to tell you what is *right*. Saddle up, hitch up, gather your critters and drift on.'

When Jethro finished speaking he stood

21

there looking at Handley and McElroy. Above and behind him swarthy King Lewis with that shotgun balanced across his lap, backed up old Jethro's quiet, corn-husk dry words with an unwaveringly menacing look.

Hoyt started to speak. Graeme cut across his first word. 'Never mind, boys. Never mind anything at all. I don't want to hear what you've got to say; no threats an' no promises. Just load up an' pull out.'

'And if we don't?' said Buck, studying that rock-jawed older man. 'What then?'

'You will. You will because you're neither of you fools. There is a lot of country between here and the Tetons; lots of good grass. You don't particularly need the Devil's Punch Bowl and I do.'

'We're satisfied right here, Mister Graeme.'

King Lewis's oily stare left Hoyt to stay unblinkingly upon Handley. It was as though Lewis wished to permanently fix that face in his mind.

Jethro let a moment pass before speaking again. He looked out and around where those distant, motionless riders sat, then onward down around the wagon-camp where other still figures stood. His stare was inhospitable and as thoughtfully speculative as the look of a general in an enemy's camp might be. 'Boys,' he eventually said, in that same soft, clipped way of speaking which marked him as a man who was minimal in speech, 'I'd like for it to end right here. But that's up to you.' He turned, retrieved his horse from JG's rangeboss, mounted and said from a greater height. 'I know you have twenty men. I also recognise your toughness. But sometimes men make mistakes about other men. Don't underestimate *my* toughness.'

Handley's judgement of this craggy old man was that he never bluffed, never turned the other cheek, and never took a backward step. Remembering the daughter he could easily see where she got that quiet depth of iron strength she'd shown him earlier this same day.

At Buck's side lanky Hoyt seemed to relinquish all interest in old Graeme and put his own attention upon the dark JG foreman and to a lesser extent upon the men around him. He recognised young Billy Curtin among them; Billy was white from throat to eyes but those other riders were not nearly as apprehensive as they were warily watchful. It was an awkward time.

'There's plenty of land here, Mister Graeme,' said Buck Handley. 'More than enough for us both.'

'I'm not going to argue with you,' said old Jethro in a wintry tone. 'Everything we could say has been said many times before between my kind and your kind. I'm not going to wait a week for you to make up your mind, either. Get out of the Devil's Punch Bowl.'

Jethro took up his reins, shot another look

onward and outward, turned his horse and started away. Buck stood with the yellow sun burning against him from a brassy-faded sky saying nothing, not moving, keeping his gaze fixed upon those retreating riders.

Eventually Hoyt McElroy murmured: 'I know the kind. I know 'em well. Some try reason; some don't say a word, just hit a camp in the night with everythin' they got. But *that* kind, Buckley my boy, they're the worst. They give a man fair warnin', then if necessary they bankrupt themselves makin' good what they say. That old devil's poison four ways from the middle.'

'But he's got the handsomest daughter you ever saw,' said Handley as he started back towards the wagons.

McElroy looked after him. He called out: 'Hey; where did you meet any girls up in here?'

Buck was flagging those outlying riders in. He said over his shoulder, 'Up a sidehill trail this morning. It was only one girl—not girls. She was that old devil's daughter.'

The men gathered and stood close listening to Hoyt repeat what had been said. It was no less than they expected; rangeriders didn't hire out to the free-graze men unless they were reconciled to trouble and willing to meet it head-on. One of the riders, a man named Fred Naylor, put his narrowed look on the river and across it to the nearest hilltops. He said he thought they should keep sentries out day and night after this. Hoyt agreed and detailed Naylor and a buckaroo named Art Waters to take the first watch. These two went wordlessly to their horses, mounted and rode off through the dancing heat.

'The balance o' you,' directed Hoyt, 'alternate out with the cattle. And, boys, keep a sharp watch. Don't go ridin' near no man-high boulders nor brush patches. I'm not sayin' JG will pot-shoot you, but a wise man don't take no risks either.'

The cowboys broke up, some walking into shade, some heading for their horses. Hoyt went along to where Buck was standing alone in thought. 'Everything's set,' Hoyt reported. 'Sentry's been sent out an' the men'll stay with the herd. 'Can't do much more until we know what old iron-bottom's got in mind.' Hoyt began making a cigarette. Beside him Handley shook out of his reverie and watched the smoke take shape.

'I've been thinkin', Hoyt. The last three, four years the pressure on free-grazers has been increasing.'

'Yup,' agreed Hoyt, lighting up.

'The land's filling up. That's why.'

'Seems that way all right, Buck.' Hoyt had as yet no idea what Handley was coming to, but he had worlds of patience so he smoked and looked far out and waited.

'It'll only be a matter of time before all the

free-graze is taken up. Homesteaded or patented or bought or filed on. Five, ten years, Hoyt.'

'Mebbe,' said McElroy, beginning to get the drift of his pardner's thoughts. 'But in five, ten years we'll have enough money to quit anyway.'

Buck peered directly at McElroy. 'Do you want to quit?' he asked.

Hoyt shook his head. 'Cattle's all I know. I teethed on a saddlehorn. 'Been punchin' cattle since I was big enough to climb up the side of a horse. When I'm mebbe a hundred years old I'll quit, but that'll be another few years yet.' Hoyt twinkled a merry look. 'How about you—you want to quit?'

'No. But I think we're overlooking something.'

'What?'

'Well; we're makin' money with our herds, but things are changing around us, Hoyt, and we're not changin' with 'em. We're goin' on as we've done since the war ended. We've been operatin' as though everything was always going to remain as it was when we started.'

Hoyt began to meticulously study the ragged tip of his cigarette. 'An' now you figure we ought to change with the times. Well hell; that's fine with me, Buck, only just how do you figure we ought to do this? You know how it is with us free-grazers: We make good money because we don't marry nothin'; we let the

26

established folks put up fences and buildings and all that; we use the grass until it's gone, then we move on to new grass.'

'That's just it,' stated Buck. 'Naturally I don't think we're as wrong for operatin' that way as the established cowmen swear we are— but I've been standing here thinking that right or wrong isn't the important thing any more. What *is* important, Hoyt, is that unless we *do* acquire good land pretty quick now, the day is fast approachin' when all the worthwhile land will be taken up and we'll be frozen out entirely.'

'How could they keep us off?' Hoyt asked.

'By fencing. They're already doing it. Yeah I know, the fence-builders are far east of us yet, but you've seen that wire with the barbs on it, Hoyt; you know how each year the stuff is being strung farther and farther west.'

'Progress,' murmured Hoyt, letting his cigarette fall and stomping it. 'I reckon that's what's called progress. Well; I sure as hell don't like it. What's the country comin' to— wire fences criss-crossin' it?'

Buck shrugged. 'I don't like it either,' he answered. 'But that's not going to stop it from coming.' He looked at McElroy's tough, lined and leathery countenance. 'Something I noticed years back, Hoyt—there comes a time in every man's life when change aggravates him. He can do one of two things: He can change too, or he can sit down somewhere and

27

spend his time cussin' progress. If he does the latter, why then life starts passin' him by. After a while he becomes an old man out of the whirl of things; a sort of relic.'

Hoyt lifted his face. 'You're wonderin' which I'm goin' to be; is that it?'

Buck said candidly: 'No, not exactly. You're too young to be fully settled in your ways yet, Hoyt. What I'm thinkin' is—shouldn't one of us head for the state capital and file on the Devil's Punch Bowl?'

McElroy's brows drew inward and downward. He twisted at the waist to consider the great sweep of valley land around them. For a long time he said nothing, just looked, then he ultimately faced Buck again looking solemn, and said, 'Well hell; if we got to quit ramblin', why I expect this here is as pretty an' as rich a place to do it in as any other I know of.' He grinned a little at Buck. 'All right; I'll stay with you on this idea. Maybe just so's you won't say I'm too old to change. Which one of us rides for the capital?'

'I will,' Buck said. 'I'll need a paper from you authorisin' me to withdraw money from your account to pay half the filin' fees.'

But Hoyt was turning things over in his mind, balancing and totalling; when he spoke again he also wagged his head. 'No; I'll go,' he exclaimed. 'I'll go because I know Graeme's goin' to cause trouble, an' I only know one way to cut an old devil like that down to size, an'

28

maybe that's not the best way to start out with him if we're goin' to be neighbours. Now you—I've seen you handle these old firebrands before—an' you got deeplomacy, Buckley. I think that's what's goin' to be needed here. F'that reason I'll make the ride an' take care o' the filin'. Now you—well—you do what's got to be done about old Graeme.'

Buck nodded. For some little time the two of them stood on without moving, without speaking, each busy with his own thoughts. Overhead the sun was dropping off towards the west and reddening as it did this. Heat-haze, like odourless smoke, obscured the highest peaks and sifted lower, over the valley itself, softening the glare a little but not minimising the warmth one bit.

Finally McElroy said forcefully: 'Damn,' and added nothing to it. But it was an eloquently spoken epithet full of clear meaning.

Buck understood and nodded. He turned towards the wagon-camp with Hoyt at his side. They paced along quietly and halted where old Burton Riddle, their camp-cook, was scowlingly at work under a texas, with streams of sweat dripping into a cooking fire from his chin.

'Make me a bundle,' ordered Hoyt, speaking to Riddle.

The cook swung around testily. 'Some reason you can't eat when everyone else does?' he irritably demanded.

Hoyt put a squinty look forward. 'Burton,' he said in that deceptively mild way of his, 'why don't you just make me the bundle and leave off all the cussin' an' rantin' because you and I both know you're goin' to make it up anyway.'

Burton Riddle, a crippled ex-cowboy, stiffened here and there from sleeping too many years upon wet ground, shot Buck a look of purest exasperation. 'It ain't hot enough just doin' the reg'lar work; now it's in-between snacks too. I got a notion to . . .'

Buck interrupted. 'Burt; we've been together a long time. Since the war in fact. How many times have Hoyt or I asked for special consideration?'

Riddle growled a fierce oath under his breath, flung perspiration off and whipped around presenting his back to McElroy and Handley, who exchanged a long-suffering look but said nothing.

The dying day was totally silent except for an occasional bawl far out where a cow hunted a calf or a heifer sought a bull. That hanging haze turned faintly pink and far off in the west where the sun was sinking, a solitary black stone upthrust stood out higher and sharper than all the other peaks.

Beyond camp the San Juan, chocolate-coloured and sluggishly oily, lapped at its low banks. There were some willow clumps along here but not many, for in the snowed-in

30

winters these were the only tender shoots elk and deer and antelope found to eat; they kept too many willows from growing.

Standing together loosely, watching their men out where the cattle were, McElroy and Handley had little to speak of which they had not already discussed. But as all men are influenced by their moods, McElroy said, 'Buck; be careful. We don't know what Graeme can do. We don't know this country too well either. Be real careful until I get back. Maybe I can make the ride in six days, round-trip.'

'I'll be careful,' said Buck. 'If there's a way around old Graeme I'll take it. Only I don't think there is. You saw him; you heard him talk.'

'Watch out for stampedes in the night. Keep remindin' the boys about gettin' bushwhacked.'

Buck turned; he smiled. 'You'd make a good mother,' he said.

Burton Riddle came limping from beneath his texas. 'Here's your bundle,' he rumbled at Hoyt. 'Hope you choke on it.'

Hoyt took it saying, with a wink at Buck, 'I wish you well too, you crabby old devil.'

CHAPTER FOUR

Hoyt left before sundown but close to it; he told Buck he wished to get out of the mountains before full dark, and yet he did not start earlier because of the insufferable heat in the canyons and passes he must travel through.

Buck saw him off. They shook hands and grinned a little at one another, for this was the way it was. A man never knew upon the plains or in the mountains whether he would ever again see friends upon earth.

A new pair of watchers took their blankets, their guns and some food, and rode out to relieve the afternoon sentries upon a westerly hillock across the river where there was a good long view of the entire valley. Other men drifted in from patrolling the herd, replaced at this chore by designated night-hawks. By the time Buck saw Hoyt fade out in the smoky late afternoon Burton Riddle was busy making supper and all the other details of camp life had been attended to. The men turned out their mounts, dumped their saddles nearby and sauntered into camp-shade looking dry and leathery and dark-shirted from sweat. Buck saw Fred Naylor looking at him and knew something was on Naylor's mind. He waited there, knowing it would come out eventually. It did ultimately come out but it was a considerable time coming. Fred worked up a smoke, sauntered over where Buck was lounging, waiting for Burton Riddle to sing out, and said casually, 'Something's been pesterin' me all day, an' until 'bout a half hour ago I didn't get it worked out.'

Buck looked mildly at Naylor, saying nothing.

'That black-lookin' cuss with Graeme this mornin'. The one sittin' up there with the scatter-gun in his lap.'

'Lewis,' said Buck. 'Graeme called him King Lewis. He's the JG rangeboss; at least I got that impression.'

'Well,' muttered Naylor, 'names never meant much to me. Y'know how it is—they come an' they go, an' who ever remembers their names. But that one—I remember him all right. Only it took me near all day to do it.'

'What about him?'

'Right after the war Texas Ben Thompson's brother shot and killed the sheriff at Abilene. You recollect hearin' about that?'

'Yes. The sheriff wasn't armed and the governor of Kansas put a bounty on Billy Thompson.'

'That black-lookin' feller—that there King Lewis—he was one of the bounty hunters that went down into Texas, found Billy, and snuck him out o' Texas an' back to Kansas. He got two thousand dollars for that.'

Buck slowly frowned over at Naylor. 'How

33

do you know Lewis did that?' he demanded.

'Easy,' answered Naylor. 'I was one o' the deputy lawmen who was there to take Billy Thompson over when this here Lewis brought him in. That's what's been pesterin' me all day, Buck. I knew blamed well I'd seen that feller somewhere before, an' I knew it wasn't good—whatever I couldn't recollect 'bout him. Then it come to me just as I was fixin' to ride on into camp from out yonder. That's him all right; maybe I forget names but I don't ever forget faces—especially one as black an' mean-lookin' as his.'

Buck said nothing for a while, considering what Naylor had revealed about JG's rangeboss. The last he'd heard, Billy Thompson had been tried and acquitted for that old killing, on the grounds that it was accidental. He now thought that Lewis must also know this, as well as how vindictive the Thompson brothers were, and that would account for him being this far from the Texas trails.

'I don't reckon he's using the same name he was using then, Fred,' said Buck. 'And as far as that goes we're not concerned. But now we know one thing about JG—they've got a killer on the payroll, and that *does* concern us—all of us. So you pass the word among the boys. Tell them if they see Lewis anywhere not to turn their backs on him.'

'Sure enough,' assented Naylor. 'But what

I've been thinkin'—if Graeme hired him, then Graeme might also know, an' if he does . . .'

Naylor let it trail off, his meaning clear enough. Buck heeded this innuendo and in retrospect tried to determine from recollection whether Jethro Graeme was capable of the things King Lewis was clearly and obviously capable of, too.

'I don't know,' he softly said aloud. 'I just plain don't know. He's hard as iron, that much you can read in his face. But the other—I just plain don't know.' Buck straightened up. 'Still; we'll take no chances. You pass the word, Fred.'

'All right. One more thing, Buck. When I was a few miles down-country this afternoon seein' how far our critters had drifted, I spied sunlight up in the westerly rocks reflectin' off metal—a gun barrel maybe or a silver bit of belt-buckle. I didn't go over to investigate, but none of our men would have any reason to ride up that pass, out of the valley, and top-out among them high peaks.'

'They're watching us all right,' said Buck, not greatly concerned. 'Graeme'll have men keeping an eye on us to see whether we obey his edict and pull out or not.'

'And—are we?'

'Going to pull out? No, Fred, we're not.'

Naylor departed, walking back where the riders were squatting, talking desultorily among themselves and eating. Buck watched

35

him go; he did not at once join his men but instead went out a little ways from camp and put a thoughtful gaze south-eastward where that pass lay through which the JG men had ridden that morning. He had no idea what lay beyond the break in the granite ramparts which encircled the Devil's Punch Bowl, but he thought that perhaps within the next day or two, if nothing occurred to deter him, he'd take a ride out that pass and look over the country beyond.

Later, after he'd eaten and was idly watching a monte game under one of the canvasses, along with a number of his men, he was abruptly alerted to something out of the ordinary by a trilling Indian call from on across the river where the brace of sentries were.

Someone among the monte players made one slashing, instinctive sweep with an arm to strangle the candles by which the gamblers had been playing. After that, men stepped well away from that spot moving out and around in the soft-lighted night.

'Fred,' called Buck softly. 'You an' Percy Devlin come with me.'

A pair of lean shadows moved forward. They came in behind Buck and trailed him as he paced westerly towards the river. A man loomed up there mounted on his horse. He recognised Buck and leaned down to quietly say, 'We seen him just a little bit ago. First, we heard him comin'. He's astride a shod horse.'

'You sure he's not one of the nighthawks?' asked Buck.

The man from that hillock across the San Juan bent a sardonic look at Buck. 'Plumb sure,' he said, brusquely. 'We know where all our fellers are. No, sir; this here feller's not one o' us.' The rider straightened up and pointed. 'He's comin' on in from the south. He's ridin' like he's got a purpose for bein' here too.'

Buck started away from the sentinel. Fred Naylor and Percy Devlin, a wide-shouldered and narrow-hipped Texan with a knife-scarred face and straw-blond hair, moved out silently behind him. Fred had a saddle carbine with him but Devlin had only his holstered six-gun. They hadn't walked more than a thousand yards before Buck abruptly halted, threw up an arm for silence, and stood there listening to the unhurried cadence of a ridden horse approaching. He dropped down to one knee. Behind him Naylor and Devlin did the same. All three of them skylined that rider long before they were in turn seen.

Fred hunched forward to speak lowly to Buck. 'I recognise him; he was with old Graeme this mornin'.'

Buck let the rider get within fifty before rising up off the ground directly ahead of the man. At sight of him the stranger's horse gave a loud snort and shied violently sideways. Before the rider had his mount completely under control Buck, Fred and Percy Devlin

37

were around him. He looked owlishly at the trio of them, for a space of time unable or unwilling to speak. Finally he said, 'Any o' you fellers Mr. Handley?'

Buck nodded. 'I am,' he said. 'What about it?'

The cowboy raised a hand to put it inside his levi jumper. At once Percy Devlin cocked his Winchester. That moving hand became utterly motionless. In a complaining voice the rider said: 'Hell's bells, I'm on'y reachin' for a letter I fetched along fer Mr. Handley.' He kept his protesting glance upon Devlin until Buck spoke.

'Easy, Perc; if he's got a letter let him get it. If he goes for a gun—he'd have to be an awful fool with these odds against him.'

The cowboy finished rummaging inside his jumper. He brought forth a white envelope, handed it down to Buck and looked over at Fred and Percy Devlin. 'That's all I'm supposed to do,' he said. 'Deliver you that there letter an' get back to the ranch as quick as I can.'

'Back to JG?' asked Naylor.

'Yeah; back to JG.'

Buck was peering closely at the letter; it was not light enough to make out more than his name written across the envelope's front in a bold, graceful hand. He gave it up, glanced at the cowboy and nodded.

'Go on,' he said. 'Head out if you want to.'

The three of them started back to camp.
Buck holding the letter carelessly. They halted
once, where they encountered that mounted
sentinel.

'Hear him?' Buck asked.

The horseman said, 'Yeah; he's goin' back a
little faster than he come on. What'd he want?'

Buck gestured with the envelope. 'It's all
right for now, I guess, but keep a close watch.'
He passed along with Devlin and Naylor
beside him.

Back at the wagons men were standing
around looking out into the soft night saying
very little and waiting. When Buck strode
among them he made a second motion with
the envelope. Here, Percy Devlin and Fred
Naylor split off; they headed for the cook-fire.
Men crowded up to ask them what it was all
about.

Buck went to a hanging lantern, lit it and
opened his envelope. The letter was brief and
the signature belonged to Kate Graeme. She
asked that he meet her the next morning
where they had initially met. That was all; no
warning, no appeal, no threat—only that
request for a meeting.

He stood a while trying to guess the reason
behind the letter, then he pocketed it, went
over to silently and thoughtfully eat his supper,
and afterwards to seek his bedroll. Whatever
Kate Graeme wished of him, he'd find out
soon enough.

CHAPTER FIVE

When dawn came with its gradually widening pale blue streakedness, its fresh new air and its good coolness, Buck rode out of camp. He was several hours early for the meeting with Kate Graeme and he meant it to be this way.

Where a game trail angled up along a flinty barranca he reached the first low heights. Later, he crossed the pack-mule trail he'd been upon when he'd met Kate the day before. But he neither halted here nor remained upon this trail. He crossed it to a branching buck-run, rowelled his horse up this steep ascent and levelled off where the buck-run made a circling, leisurely approach to the nearest slotted pass over the top of the valley's rimrocks.

Up here where the sun had been shining for some little time it was hot, but below, in the Devil's Punch Bowl where that heat did not as yet lay, there was a misty, dawn-like shadowiness.

The land eastward and southward was all new to Buck. He dismounted, stood at his horse's head and made a long, serious study of it. A few miles south-eastward was a ranch; he could not make out anything other than the flash of light off a series of glass windows, but this was like a heliograph signal telling him what was over there.

'That,' he told his disinterested horse, 'will be old Graeme's JG outfit.'

There were no other buildings anywhere that Buck could see. The land down the far side of his vantage point ran on in an undulating way for measureless miles. It was good land with tough grass and wiry browse. There were occasional spits of trees, pines and firs, and infrequently brush clumps, mostly sage and chapparal, but otherwise the land was mostly open, grassed-over and as good as any cattle country he'd ever seen.

He alternated between studying JG's range outside the Punch Bowl, and the land down in the valley. It stuck in his mind that with all his other range, Jethro Graeme could give up the Devil's Punch Bowl without missing it at all.

He smiled bitterly and said to his horse: '*Could* give it up. Could but won't. They never change and mostly they never learn—those old mossbacks.'

He stepped up, eased out southward and rode a mile to a descending trail which he took and held to all the downward way to the flat land west of JG. Once, he saw a rider dusting it along parallel to him but over a mile eastward. He paused to watch this person. The rider made a long sweep through morning's dazzling sunlight curving towards the distant ranch buildings. Handley abandoned his vigil and went along until he could see where that

41

natural southerly pass led from JG's outside range down through the mountains into the Devil's Punch Bowl. This was the way Jethro Graeme had come into the valley. Here too, the ground showed from its disturbed condition that for a number of years riders and cattle had come and gone over this route.

The sun was burning now with the force of a distant, steady flame. Dust-scent hung in the air and the sky was fading out to a blue-yellow brassiness. It struck Handley that this outside range dried out much sooner than the valley did; he attributed this to those shielding high rimrocks that encircled the valley, eliminating at least two hours of sunlight each summer day.

He found a waterhole which someone had recently cleaned, watered his animal there, tanked up himself, then went over where a lonely cottonwood stood, sat down with his back to the tree's smooth trunk and worked up a cigarette.

A bone-dry creek bed meandered southerly away from the waterhole, evidently the course winter rains and overflow from the seepage spring took, when there was a residue of water. He sat there in the depthless silence fitting together in his mind what he'd observed thus far of JG, its owner, its riders, and its owner's daughter.

He also thought of Hoyt McElroy, riding somewhere northward, beyond the canyons by this time. Something Hoyt had once said came to mind and he faintly smiled. Hoyt was a good man to tie to, which could not be said of very many men. He remembered how they'd met, not long after the war, and how they'd pooled slim purses to start their first free-graze herd. In those lean, hard days Hoyt had never forgotten how to smile, which meant a lot. He'd never pushed for trouble either, but neither had he ever turned away from it.

They'd had their ups and downs; it had not been easy to accumulate a stake. But they'd done it and as far as he could now determine, neither of them had changed. This question of changing brought him to other thoughts; to a long assessment of what they were now embarking upon. There would be trouble over this. He knew that as well as he knew night followed day. But he reasoned that this would be their last fight; once they had title to their valley and were established there, being legally right would end the strife. Animosity would perhaps remain—Jethro Graeme's iron-jawed image cropped up here—but time would take care of that. Time was a great healer.

He killed the smoke, stood up, slanted a look at the sun, decided it was time to meet Kate Graeme, or shortly would be, and took two steps forward towards his horse.

A sharp voice hit him hard in the back.

'Steady, mister. Stand just like you are. Don't turn around.'

Surprise more than any other emotion turned Handley to stone in mid-stride. He thought he knew that voice but was not sure. 'All right,' he growled. 'It's your move.'

'Shuck your gun.'

Buck drew his pistol and let it fall. He then began to very slowly reverse his stand. No order came prohibiting this. He was separated by a hundred feet from the dark, fierce face of JG's rangeboss, King Lewis.

'You must be part Indian,' he exclaimed. 'I didn't hear you at all.'

Lewis let this pass. He had an uncocked six-gun in his fist over which he studied Handley. 'I was lookin' over some waterholes to see if our riders had cleaned them yesterday like I said for 'em to. I spied you sittin' up among the rimrocks and trailed you down here. What d'you want out here; what you sneakin' aroun' for?'

'Any law against a man getting the lay of the country hereabouts?'

'For you there might be. Graeme told you to make a gather and get out of here. Why aren't you gone?'

'For one thing,' replied Buck, 'you don't round up three thousand head of cattle in a couple of days. For another . . .'

'You haven't made any attempt to round up them critters, Handley. I know. I been watchin' you fellers from the rims.'

Buck looked down at the uncocked six-gun.

44

'Use it or put it up,' he said. 'I'm disarmed; what more do you need?'

Lewis was silent; he glowered but Buck got the feeling that something was holding him back. He thought it had to be some order Jethro Graeme had given him, otherwise, from what Naylor had told him about this swarthy big man, and what he could read in Lewis's face, that gun would have been fired by now. He relaxed where he stood putting faith in this tenuous judgement, giving Lewis look for look.

'Are you goin' to pull out, or aren't you?' Lewis demanded.

'Why don't you wait and see,' retorted Buck. He bent down, scooped up his six-gun, stood for a moment with it lying loose in his hand exchanging a wintry look with JG's rangeboss, then dropped the weapon into his hip-holster. Lewis said nothing about this nor took his hostile glare off Buck.

'I'm beginning to understand something about you,' Buck said, catching at the reins of his mount, drawing the animal to him. 'A lot of men have the same trouble—you can't make a quick decision.' He deliberately turned his back, toed into a stirrup and rose up to settle over leather. When he faced Lewis again he saw that the uncocked six-gun was sagging a little. 'I'll give you a little advice too,' he said from the saddle. 'I'm surprised you don't already know it. Don't point an uncocked gun at a man, Lewis.'

45

The rangeboss holstered his weapon and started forward. He was large and powerful. 'For your kind I don't need no gun,' he snarled, halting a few feet from Handley. 'Now I'll give you some advice! Get those damned pothook cattle out of the valley before day after tomorrow or I'll be along with some riders an' put 'em out!'

Buck said gently: 'Seven JG riders against twenty free-grazers? That'd be right foolish, Lewis. But if you're of a mind to try it—come ahead. We'll be waiting.'

'Not seven, Handley, fifty. Graeme's already sent for more men. They'll be here by day after tomorrow. Put *that* in your damned pipe an' smoke it!'

Buck sat on gazing into the hot black eyes of King Lewis seeing defiance in every line of the man's big body. Without another word he turned his horse and rode away. Once, where the pass ran between overhead flanges of raw, weathered granite, he turned to look back. Lewis was no longer in sight. He paused here to make another smoke, light it and sit quiet for a time, the heat forgotten, the hating eyes of JG's rangeboss forgotten, thinking only of that revelation: Was it true? He had only to recall that iron-visaged old man's face to know that it was. He took up his reins eventually and rode on, down into the pass where bitter dust jerked up under his horse and the strong odour of many cattle drives came to him.

He came to the branch-off he knew by instinct would be somewhere close. Here, the main, wide, old and beaten trail led down into the Devil's Punch Bowl. On his right, northward, was the cut-off where that lesser trail went. He took this turn, went along a half mile before stubbing out his cigarette upon the saddlehorn, tilting back his head and running a close look upward. He had not passed Kate nor had he seen her precede him through the pass; this meant she had come, if indeed she was ahead of him at all, over the rim.

She had; he found the game trail she'd used and read the sign of her passing, A little ways beyond, where a scowling obsidian out-thrust forced the trail to make a long-spending curve, he came riding around and saw her ahead of him seated upon a smooth boulder looking down into the valley.

Here, there was a weak kind of shade. Here too, probably caused by air currents passing upwards from the valley below as well as from over the rim, there was a rustling little breath of disturbed air. She turned as he came along, looked over without speaking and let him dismount, drop his reins and step forward, then she stood up.

Her face was still at his approach. He searched for expression, found only a shadow of scepticism as she viewed him, a very faint look of appraisal, then she turned to resume gazing out over the huge valley below them where riders and cattle were tiny and heat-hazed. He stopped at her side saying, 'Let me guess why you sent that note. Your father sent for more men and you'd like to head off the trouble that's coming, if you can.'

She swung towards him, her green eyes emerald-dark and probing. 'How did you know that?' she demanded.

'I met your foreman near the pass. He told me.'

She turned this over in her mind. 'I suppose he did at that,' she eventually murmured. 'My father didn't and I didn't. King was the only other person who knew.'

'Thanks,' Buck said dryly. 'If I have to be called a liar I like the way you do it better than most folks.'

'Anyway, you're right. I don't want trouble to come. Not *that* kind of trouble.'

'What kind is *"that"*?'

'You know well enough. Gun-trouble. Shooting and killing.'

'That could be easy to avoid. Tell Lewis an' your father to keep those hired guns out of the Devil's Punch Bowl. There won't be any trouble then.'

Her brows curved inward a little and downward. Seeing this, Buck thought again of the hauteur he'd seen in her before. When she would have spoken he reached up, thumbed back his hat, put a grave glance outward and downward into the valley, and said, 'Miss Kate;

48

it's pretty hard to have trouble unless both sides want it. My side doesn't want it.'

'Then leave. Round up your cattle and move along.'

He shook his head at her, looking around. 'No; I don't figure to do that. Particularly when someone orders me to.'

'Then you'll have trouble. Bad trouble, Mister Handley. My father is not an easy man.'

Buck nodded over this. 'I saw that yesterday. But you know, Miss Kate, there's something folks have a habit of overlookin'. They get so wrapped up in themselves—in how *they* feel, how *they* react, how *they* think things should be, that they almost always forget to consider the other person.'

'Are you trying to tell me that you're not an easy man either, Mister Handley?'

'Exactly that, ma'm. I don't want trouble with JG. But I haven't walked away from a fight since Appomattox.'

'No,' said Kate Graeme bitterly, turning away from him again. 'And I can guess which side you were on then, too.'

'That wouldn't be hard, ma'm, seeing that I'm a Texan.'

'Do you like being on the losing side in your fights, Mister Handley?'

Buck thinly smiled. 'In *that* fight, ma'm, I was on the side that won every battle—and lost the war.'

'It can happen like that again. I rode all the

49

way over here to ask you not to let it come to this.'

'Well now, ma'm,' drawled Buck, 'seems to be you could have served yourself better if you'd stayed at JG and spent this same effort talkin' to your pappy.'

'I talked to him.'

Buck, watching her profile, said, 'I see. And it didn't do any good there either. Is that it?'

'You're right, it didn't do a particle of good. I'd hoped, since you're younger, you might not be so bull-headed.'

'A common enough mistake to make,' he told her, soft and final, stepped closer and also studied the soft-shaded landfall below them, felt that little roiled air upon his face and felt too, the powerful magic of her closeness.

'There've been times in my life when I've wished I didn't have to do what I had to do; this is one of them.'

She didn't move, she only said softly, 'Why?'

That one word threw him off a little in his solemn thinking. 'Why?' he said, looking sharply at her, then drifting his glance away again. 'Well; because I hate the idea of you an' me being on opposite sides, I guess. And for other reasons too. Few men in this world really want to fight other men. It takes a lot of time, never really settles anything, and sometimes it cuts a man down in his prime an' he never achieves any of his goals in life.'

'True,' she said, still without looking around

at him. 'It's a beautiful valley, isn't it?'

'Very beautiful, yes.'

'But it isn't worth getting cut down for, is it? I mean, there are other beautiful valleys, Mister Handley. Other places where a man can work towards the things he wants in life.' She made a little fluttering motion with one hand. 'What good is all that beauty if you're buried under six feet of it—no good at all.'

'I reckon when I was philosophising I left something out, Miss Kate.'

'What?'

'Well; you said I was on the losing side during the war, and that's plumb right, I was. But what I forgot to mention was that men have ideals. They cherish them and if they're men with feeling, ma'm, they don't regret dying for them.'

'Death is so final, Mister Handley. What ideal could you possibly have where the Devil's Punch Bowl is concerned? You only saw it a day or two ago.'

'It's not the valley, ma'm, it's being ordered off. It's also being threatened by a man like Lewis, being thrown down on from behind. And it's also being denied a right which I possess to run cattle in here if I can.'

She slowly turned now, her face very still, her eyes totally unmoving. 'Are you saying King drew a gun on you, Mister Handley?' she demanded.

'Yes'm, he did. I rode over on your side of

51

the rim earlier this morning. I was careless; it was hot and near the pass I sat down near a waterhole. When I rose up later to ride on down here an' meet you—there he was, right behind me with his gun out and ready. That's how I learned about those fifty men JG is gettin' up into a war party against us.'

For a moment Kate was silent. Ultimately she said, 'I want to apologise for King. That was a bad thing to do and a bad time to do it.'

'Why a bad time, ma'm?'

'Because I want you to leave. I want you to do that for your own sake. Don't bow your back over what King did. If it'll salve your pride, Mister Handley, I'll make him ride over here and apologise in person for that stupidity of his.'

Buck studied her; he could not believe that this beautiful girl could order a man of King Lewis's type to do anything which Lewis would do. 'Never mind,' he said to her, with less than three feet separating them. 'Never mind Lewis. He wouldn't apologise, but even if he did, he wouldn't mean it. I know his kind possibly better than you do, Miss Kate. Next time he won't get that close, I promise you that.'

They stood looking steadily at one another. Kate's gaze neither wavered nor dropped away. Her straining blouse rose and fell and a sturdy pulse beat in her creamy throat.

'You won't leave,' she murmured, making a statement of it.

52

'No, ma'm.'

'Maybe your pardner would, if I spoke to him.'

'If anyone could speak to Hoyt and make him come around it would be you, ma'm. But I'm afraid you can't do it now.'

'Now? What do you mean?'

'He left the valley yesterday.'

'Ahhh; I see. To get more men. Mister Handley, I misjudged you. I thought, when we first met, you were not typical of your kind.' Kate started to move around Buck. 'I made a mistake.'

He reached out to catch her arm, to swing her back towards him. 'The only mistake you made was to come to me, a stranger, instead of making your father listen to reason.' He would have said more but she looked icily at his detaining hand upon her arm, then up into his face.

'Take your hand off me,' she said very gently, in a voice as dry as rattling corn husks.

Buck obeyed; let his arm fall back to his side. They stood like that watching each other, and without any encouragement at all, a confused and confusing emotion suddenly came into the charged atmosphere around them. Buck felt it and he also saw it mirrored in the depths of Kate's eyes.

She swung abruptly, went to her horse, mounted and reined away without once looking back.

CHAPTER SIX

It was high noon the next day when the sentry upon his little hillock on across the river signalled with a piece of glass. There was one blinding white flash, a pause, another white flash. That was all, but among the wagons where Handley's nighthawks were drowsing underneath wagons in full shade, a ripple of quick talk erupted.

Old Burton Riddle grunted down from inside a wagon, craned eastward, saw those signals repeated and hobbled swiftly over where a steel skillet hung. He grabbed up a ladle and struck the skillet four times, hard. That ringing sound carried in all directions nearly as far as the hills. From far out riders began loping stiffly in from the herd. Among them was Buck; when he slid down to a halt Riddle pointed wordlessly with his ladle over where the looking-glass signals were being flashed at regular intervals. Riders bunched up near Riddle's texas, some mounted, some on foot holding reins, others, part of the alternate crew which was resting at camp, barefooted and tousel-headed from sleep.

'Horsemen comin',' a short and massive cowboy named Buff Evans said. 'Must be quite a mob of 'em the way Perc's signallin'. What you want us to do, Buck?'

54

Handley turned. 'Those of you that're mounted go on out and warn the other men with the cattle. Get into groups of no less than threes. Don't let any strangers get within rifle-shot of you, and watch no one tries to stampede the cattle. The rest of you—go on back to your rest or whatever you were doing. Just keep a sharp eye on things and a hand on your Winchesters. If it's old Graeme again he won't be out for blood—not yet. Not in the middle of the day when he knows we'll be forewarned of his coming.'

The cook said sourly: 'One time I mis-read a man like Graeme.' He tapped a crippled leg. 'I got a good memento of that mistake.'

Buck got back astride as the other riders began bending away. He called to a tobacco-chewing, rough and wiry-looking man called Laramie Potter saying, 'Laramie; you and Curt come along with me.'

The three of them spurred over into a lope and went southward paralleling the San Juan until they saw that body of horsemen the watcher had signalled was approaching. When Buck stopped, Curt Walker said quietly: 'A damned sight more'n seven of 'em this time.'

It was not possible immediately to discern Jethro Graeme among the heat-hazed, close-bunched riders, but when they were close enough to slow a little Buck made him out. He also made out King Lewis at his side; Lewis again had that sawed-off shotgun balanced over his lap.

'War party,' breathed Laramie Potter, and spat aside. ''Pears to me the old gent's got some gen-u-wine gunfighters with him this time.'

Buck was thinking the same thing as he studied the oncoming men. JG's regular hands were among that party, but there was at least another full dozen of strangers; mostly, these newcomers had the sixshooter-stamp on them.

Jethro drew rein facing Buck and as before when he did this he dropped both hands upon his saddlehorn. Jethro had his stiff-brimmed, low-crowned hat tilted so that it shaded both narrowed eyes. His riders crowded up on his left and on his right. They too looked hard ahead holding silent. Only King Lewis showed much expression; King looked exultant; he was near to mirthlessly smiling.

With no preliminaries and minimising his speech as was his custom, Jethro said to Buck Handley: 'You're not showing very good judgement. You should have your camp struck by today an' your cattle bunched for the trail.'

Buck sat there saying nothing, running his gaze over the gunmen among Graeme's entourage, counting their numbers and assessing their looks.

'I want you to tell me, Handley, when you're going to pull out. I want you to tell me that right now.'

'And,' said Buck, focusing his full attention

upon Graeme, 'if I tell you I'm not pulling out—what then, Mister Graeme?'

Jethro digested this. 'I think you can guess why these other men are with me,' he said. 'You're not going to be foolish are you, Handley, because if you are—you'll live long enough to regret it.'

There were twenty JG riders counting Jethro Graeme. The coincidence of this many men—the same number he had—did not escape Buck. He knew what he was going to say next and he also knew what Graeme's answer would be.

'These are better odds, Mister Graeme—for you.'

'Even better than you think, Handley,' came back that prompt exclamation. 'This will be one half of my crew by day after tomorrow. The odds will then be better than two-to-one against your free-grazers.'

Buck looped his reins and sat easy in the saddle. 'Fifty men,' he said. 'I know. I've heard that twice today.' He watched Lewis as he made this remark. Lewis's brows ran inward in a faint, puzzled way. He knew of only one person who had said this to Handley and it was plainly bothering him trying to imagine who that second person was. Buck did not tell him.

'I took a ride this morning, Mister Graeme; I saw your range beyond the Devil's Punch Bowl. I could tell by the condition of the feed

57

that the number of cattle you run don't make a dent in your JG grass. This valley isn't critical to your operation.'

'It will be,' Graeme shot back. 'It will be because there never was a free-graze range-hog who didn't start out easy, then over-run the whole countryside. You're going out of the Devil's Punch Bowl with your pothook critters and your border-scum riders, or you're going to stay here. But if you stay, Handley, it's going to be in your grave.'

'You don't own this land, Mister Graeme, it's free-graze.'

'I have prior rights here. I've run herds in here for twenty years. I have the right of use and the right of control. Handley; among decent cattlemen anywhere in the West, those are recognised and respected rights. But damned if I'll argue that with you or anyone like you. Now I want an answer from you—yes or no—are you going to pull out?'

Every eye was on Buck now. Even his own men were shallowly breathing awaiting his reply to that ultimatum.

He shook his head giving Jethro Graeme stare for stare. 'No, sir, I am not going to pull out.'

For a second King Lewis looked like he might raise his scattergun. Old Graeme's slitted eyes and tough-set lips did not alter an iota for a moment. After a strained interval he said quietly, 'It's your bed, Handley. You've just made it and now by God you're going to sleep in it.'

'One more thing,' exclaimed Buck. 'Before you turn these gunmen loose, Graeme, think a long time. This won't be the first battle I've fought. Maybe it won't be the last despite what you think. I don't want to fight you. To keep from that I'd do almost anything—but not leave the Devil's Punch Bowl. If it comes now every man around us today will know I did my part in trying like hell to prevent it.'

'Prevent it,' snarled King Lewis, fire-points of fury in his glare. 'Damn you, Handley—you come in here deliberately to make a fight with JG.'

'That,' said Buck coldly, 'is a damned lie.'

From among those bunched-up men a sound almost like a sigh passed up; the West's blood-stained soil held in its ageless grip the body of many men who had called other men liars.

Lewis was rigid in his saddle. Buck could almost hear his thoughts. Lewis knew he could not swing that shotgun to bear before Buck could draw and shoot. Still, Lewis had no intention at all of letting that remark pass. In the end he came to a decision. He held out his shotgun, it was taken by another JG rider, Lewis then dropped his split-reins, stepped down from the saddle and began to peel off his shell-belt and six-gun. He had a murderous look on his face.

Buck, seeing how Lewis wanted this settled, also dismounted. When he removed his gun-belt, turned to hand it up to Laramie Potter, the tobacco-chewing cowboy bent low and said, 'You got a knife? That 'breed offspring of a lousy squaw out-weighs you thirty pounds. I got a knife in my boot.'

Buck turned away from Laramie. He heard the resigned moan behind him as Potter exchanged an anguished look with Curt Walker.

'You'll keep the others out of it?' he asked old Graeme.

Jethro inclined his head. He was looking at Buck as though he grudgingly admired his courage but seriously doubted his sanity. 'Leave them fight it out,' he growled to his riders. 'Stay in your saddles and keep your hands away from your weapons.'

Lewis was a solid shape, naturally dark and burnt still darker by that fierce summer sun, as he paced ahead of his horse and the other men with Jethro Graeme. He was no taller than Buck but he was heavier, less sinewy with a sloping powerfulness to his heavy shoulders which told of exceptional strength. He was a hard one who had a blaze of troublesomeness in him that showed now from his hot and deadly eyes.

Buck watched him approach thinking that he'd known many like King Lewis, men without principles or scruples, physically brave and bullying men who would kill at the drop of a hat. Lewis was of that special frontier breed which was ruled by passion, motivated by restlessness, and possessed of a narrow, tight mind. He had the craftiness of a coyote and the disposition of a mountain lion; there was no mercy in him anywhere.

'Lewis,' he said, when the rangeboss was close enough to pause there, balancing forward on the balls of his feet, 'you want trouble so bad, you'd do anything to make it come. I've said repeatedly I don't want to fight Graeme. You're pushing hard for that. I'd like to know your real reason.'

'You,' snarled the rangeboss. 'You an' your kind—that's my real reason. Grass-hogs, range-thieves, that's what your kind is, Handley. I can't get to all of 'em, but by gawd I'll get to you.'

The need to exhibit prowess shone from Lewis's eyes; it was in the flattened, downward pull of his lips too. Without another word he lunged at Handley. He was the veteran of hundreds of these brawls and like such a veteran he did not now consider the lean, relaxed man ahead of him a serious contender at all. But this was not exclusively King Lewis's error; other men had made the same near-fatal mistake all the way from Texas to Canada.

Buck eased under that lunge, felt roiled air where a looping fist shot overhead, chopped a

61

savage strike into the rangeboss's middle, and danced clear.

Lewis came around sucking air through parted lips; that jab had hurt him. He stalked in again, both arms wide-flung this time, both sets of fingers bent talon-like. He meant now to close with Handley, to get his arms around him.

Buck sidled first one way then another way avoiding those big arms. Lewis jumped in, Buck jumped back. Lewis feinted, Buck would not be drawn forward. Lewis cursed and Buck smiled at him. Lewis dropped down flat-footed and stood there. Buck came closer warily, flicked out a little strike that stung, then, anticipating Lewis's next move, instantly jumped away again. Lewis hurled himself forward, met empty air, and let out a frustrated roar.

Buck, all those watchers who knew anything about this kind of fighting knew, was deliberately enraging his opponent. Several of them, sitting behind Jethro Graeme, growled instructions to Lewis, careful not to say too much or to make moves which old Jethro might not approve of.

Lewis abandoned all caution and ran at Buck. The lighter man evaded two of these attacks, but stood his ground at the third one and struck Lewis a crunching blow that stopped the rangeboss in mid-stride. Lewis shook his head as a range bull does in fly-time;

he sidled away instinctively until his vision cleared, then he started forward again. Buck was waiting. He had both legs wide-planted, knee-sprung and solidly set. He also had his right shoulder down behind his cocked right fist.

Lewis came in low and fast bending his head from side to side; he made a difficult target like this and at the last moment Buck tried to shift his stance, to side-step. He could not make the correction soon enough; Lewis crashed into him with those powerful wide-open arms snapping closed around Buck's middle. Back where Laramie Potter and Curt Walker sat rigidly watching, an anguished moan went up.

Buck whipped upright against the terrible pressure of those encircling arms. He arched and twisted, got one hand up and felt for Lewis's face. King was pushing his head hard against Handley's chest to shield his eyes. That searching hand though, found Lewis's nose, and higher, his eyes, it strained there forcing Lewis's head slowly back. The breath of both battlers sounded explosive in an atmosphere of utter hush.

Lewis never once relaxed his crushing grip, not even when his head was bent far back. Buck's face turned a peculiar, splotchy blue shade. He cocked that right fist again and fired it. Lewis gasped and staggered but held on. Buck locked his hands together into one maul-like fist, brought his next blow downward with the violence of a sledge. Bone broke, claret spewed, and King Lewis's straining arms suddenly fell away.

Buck staggered. He sucked at the hot, thin air and weaved where he stood. Opposite him JG's rangeboss wilted. His eyes turned up aimlessly and his knees turned loose. He fell gently and neither rolled nor moved. Churned earth where he lay turned a dull scarlet from his wrecked face.

Behind Jethro Graeme a man said harshly: 'Here; one o' you hold m'horse.'

Before either Potter or Walker could move in the face of this fresh threat, Jethro Graeme said: 'Sit still; don't a man of you move!' He turned his greeny, chipped-ice stare upon the riders behind him. Not a one of them moved.

Buck retrieved his hat, walked over to his horse, hooked both arms around the saddle and leaned there looking across at the JG men. His shirt was in rags and sweat glistened like oil upon his upper body. He had a sullen red welt under his jaw and lower, where his ribs worked in and out, there were the clear imprints of Lewis's mighty arms. The smoky glow of battle was still in his eyes when he said to Jethro Graeme:

'Pick him up and get out of the Devil's Punch Bowl. And he's still a liar when he says I came here lookin' for trouble.' He paused to deeply breathe, then said: 'But I reckon if

64

trouble's coming, you'll know where it can find me, Mister Graeme—right here in this valley!'

Laramie Potter handed Buck his reins. Buck mounted, watched several JG riders lift limp and unconscious King Lewis and bear him along to his horse, then he and Jethro Graeme exchanged a long, silent look before Buck turned his animal and started for the wagon-camp. Behind him rode Potter and Walker, feeling triumphant but also feeling worried. They'd seen nothing in Jethro's granite expression which indicated old Graeme would not now embark upon his crusade against the free-graze men as he promised to do before the fight.

Overhead, the molten sun fed its fiery fury downward so that the land writhed under its whip-lashing scorch.

CHAPTER SEVEN

Buck was at the river washing when he heard the first gunshot. It was fully dark with no moon yet up, the day-time heat was mostly gone and his body ached from the fight with King Lewis.

He sprang upright, naked from the waist up, grabbed at his shell-belt lying close by and stood there a moment listening. Somewhere, far out, running horses made a drum-roll sound. There were two more gunshots, then the unmistakable booming roar of a shotgun. Buck started for camp in a dead-run; ahead, men were crying to one another in the darkness around the wagons. When he got close enough to make out what was happening among the wagons he saw men with Winchesters rolling out, whipping upright, dashing for the rope-corral where uneasy animals were anxiously milling.

He bawled out at those sprinting figures: 'Hold it. Come back here. Don't charge out there until we know what's going on. It could be an ambush.'

Burton Riddle came hobbling; he had an ancient Springfield army rifle in one fist, a pouch of bullets in the other hand. 'It's that damned Graeme again,' he roared. 'He's come back to finish the fight with you.'

There were seven men in camp, the balance were either out with the cattle or were down by the river doing their laundry. They came straggling over where Buck was putting on a shirt beside one of the wagons. Each of them was armed and anxious. When they began speaking Buck ordered them to be quiet. In the ensuing silence he heard a rider coming on at top speed from the south-west. He turned in that direction and started walking, pushing in the shirt-tail as he paced along. Behind him, uncertain but grim, other men also hiked along.

The horseman was Percy Devlin; at sight of Buck he slid down to a sliding halt and gestured backwards with a saddle-gun. 'Gawddamned night-riders out there,' he panted. 'There wasn't no warnin' at all. One minute I was makin' my sashay around the herd—the next minute someone took a shot at Art Waters where he was comin' around towards me. Then all hell busted loose over on the far side o' the herd.'

Buck snapped at the men with him: 'All right; get mounted. Buff; rig out my horse and fetch it back with you.'

Burton Riddle was limping towards the rope-corral too, still gripping that Springfield rifle, when Buck called him back. Burt came but he was plainly in a rebellious frame of mind, in no mood to be ordered to remain behind. When he halted he said, 'You'll need every hand you got out there.'

Buck shook his head. Another burst of angry gunfire erupted which kept him still and listening for a moment. These shots seemed to come from southward and apparently from two different parties of men.

'Now we're shootin' back,' growled Riddle, also head-cocked listening.

'Never mind that. We'll take care of the fighting,' retorted Buck. 'Burt; you take a couple of the boys and empty all but three of the wagons; hitch 'em up and drive 'em northward along the river until you come to a

67

dense tree-thicket. Hide 'em in there.'

Riddle's face twisted. 'What the hell fer?' he demanded. 'They're attackin' the . . .'

'Do as I say,' snapped Buck, seeing his cowboys approaching out of the gloom. 'They can't hurt the herd much. Use your head, Burt; they can't stampede the cattle out of the valley in the dark and they know it. So—this strike isn't aimed to put us out of the cattle business at all. It's aimed at smashing us some other way, an' there's only one way that can be done—destroy our camp an' our provisions. Now do you understand?'

Riddle's face cleared. He gradually assumed a look of admiring understanding. 'Yes, sir, Cap'n,' he briskly replied. 'I understand now. Which men'll I keep here with me?'

Buff Evans came up astride, leading Handley's saddled horse. As he held forth the reins Buck said to Riddle, 'Any two men you want.' He then swung up, waited until Riddle had chosen his men, then started out of camp with the others, hearing some disappointed oaths from the men whom Burton Riddle had selected to help him move camp.

It was dark down in the Devil's Punch Bowl. Those encircling dark mountains minimised starshine and threw their dripping dark shadows over everything. It would be some time yet before the moon rose.

Buck did not push his horse. The men around him set their gait to his, closing up on him in a bunch only when he twisted to call up two riders by name and say to them, 'Stay together, you two. Go out around the herd and locate all our men. Tell them to forget the critters for now—they can't leave the valley—and ride fast towards that southward pass Graeme's riders used getting down in here. Tell them the rest of us will be there waiting, so they'll have to be damned careful when the shooting starts.'

Some of the cowboys, up until now uncertain and perplexed by Buck's route, which was not towards the sporadic fighting at all, but which was out and around it southward, exchanged clearing looks with their companions.

The two riders broke away riding westward, staying together as they'd been ordered to do. Within moments they were entirely lost to sight in the night.

Buff Evans and Laramie Potter were on either side of Buck. Behind this trio came the other men, quiet and watchful. Now, there was only an occasional gunshot from out on the valley floor. Several times men's high yells faintly sounded, and once there was the unnerving rumble of panicked cattle in full run. A moment's study though, showed that this was only a segment of the herd.

''Be a mess if they tried a real stampede,' offered Laramie Potter to no one in particular. 'They's long nigh as many JG critters in here

69

as they is pothook animals. Old iron-faced'd have as big a loss as we'd have an' maybe more.'

Buff Evans, though, had a divergent train of thought. 'Maybe us an' old Graeme'd figure like that, but them gunhands he hired wouldn't because they don't know a JG from a pothook; all they want is excitement. Hell; they'd bust the whole passel of cattle out of here if they knew how to do it in the dark. Them kind o' fellers only care about stirrin' up something. They don't never care how they do it.'

'Shut up a minute,' complained Laramie. 'Listen. Damned if them stampedin' critters aren't headin' north, Buck, instead o' south.'

'For our camp,' exclaimed Buck, and said no more, his thoughts finding grim satisfaction in the correctness of his earlier anticipation of what those night-riders had in mind.

Behind him a cowboy with a high-pitched voice squealed indignantly: 'Damn it; how come us t'let 'em do that? Man; I got a 'spensive Mex bridle back there all slathered over with silver. It'll get stole or busted for sure.'

'You'll get paid for damage to your gatherings,' consoled Buck. 'Right now we want to get those men.'

'We could've done it at the camp,' protested the same cowboy, his tone shrill with indignation.

'No we couldn't. They'd strike and run the

cattle over us. We'd likely lose our horses, have the camp trampled, and never be able to trade more than a few shots with 'em.'

'But hell, Buck, this here . . .'

'Listen a minute,' cut in Buck testily. 'There's only one good way out of the Devil's Punch Bowl. We're headin' for it. After they think they've wrecked our camp they'll come dustin' it down to that pass. We'll be waiting for them down there.'

No one said anything for a moment. Buck used that stillness to order a gallop, and the party of them went rocketing along in the opposite direction from that northward tumult of distant sound. A considerable while later, when they slowed again, that rider with the squeaky voice proved he had a single-track mind. He sang out: 'Somebody's goin' to pay for that bridle all the same, dad burn it.'

Several men chuckled. Buck twisted to seek this man out and say, 'All right; if it's gone or busted when we get back, I'll pay for it.'

Those rearward sounds were muted by distance but still softly audible. No one spoke about them again but clearly every man was thinking of Burt Riddle and the riders who had remained behind with him, as well as their private effects back there. What ultimately drew their thoughts from these things was a sudden, sharp, night-owl cry from dead ahead through the darkness. Buck reined back at once. The cry was repeated; it was a

71

sad, mournful sound, realistic but totally unbelievable. For one thing, no owl would be anywhere close by after hearing those gunshots. For another, owls rarely night-hunted where large herds of cattle grazed.

'It's Fred Naylor,' Potter said, when the cry came again. 'He's heard us an' ain't sure which party we are.'

'I never heard Naylor make that call before,' said Buff Evans suspiciously.

'That's 'cause you never been huntin' with him,' Laramie shot right back. 'I have, an' I know that call.'

'Then ride on out there,' said Buff dourly, 'an' if you're wrong only you'll get shot up.'

'We'll all go,' said Buck, leading out.

They spread out a little and walked their animals. When a man rose up from the ground directly in Buck Handley's path half a score guns clicked in the dark, sending this chilling sound strongly ahead where that lone man stood.

'Hey, hold it,' the dark silhouette cried out. 'It's me—Naylor. Watch out with those damned guns, will you?'

'Where's your horse?' sang out Potter. 'Where's your blamed carbine, Fred?'

Naylor took a few steps forward to meet the riders closing around him. 'My horse took a full choke of buckshot from someone's danged shotgun. When he cartwheeled through the air I lost my Winchester. Ever since then I been

72

out here on foot as helpless as a babe in arms, tryin' to figure out who was who and what was what.'

'How'd you know it was us comin' along?' asked Buff Evans.

'Heard your voices,' answered Naylor, who moved over in front of Buck to say, 'Don't happen to have a spare saddle-mount in your pocket, do you, Buck?'

There were several soft chuckles over this. Buck kicked his foot clear of the stirrup, put out a downward hand and said, 'Always thought you'd look good riding squaw-style. Get up here.'

Naylor mounted. As they were lining out again he said to Buck, 'They caught a bunch of critters and stampeded 'em north.'

'Yeah,' came back a dry reply to this. Buck explained what he had in mind. After that Naylor rode along for a thoughtful time without speaking.

'We didn't have any warning at all,' he ultimately said, obviously reacting at long last to the surprise and uproar of that slashing attack. 'Damned if we did. I never even saw that feller until he let loose with his danged riot-gun.'

'You could guess who he was though, couldn't you?' asked Buck.

'Well sure; as soon as I picked myself up off the ground and got my wits together again. That black-lookin' Lewis feller. When daylight comes I'm goin' back after that saddle, an' if it's busted up Lewis's goin' to think the sky fell on him next time we cross trails.'

'You watch that damned shotgun,' rumbled Laramie Potter off to one side. 'Only way to tangle with them things is from beyond shotgun range. They make a man look like he's been through a meat grinder.'

Buck said: 'We're getting close. Laramie; ride ahead and scout the pass. I doubt if they left a man there, but make damned sure. Come back when you're satisfied; we'll be poking along.'

After Potter loped ahead the others slowed to a steady walk. Except for the abrasive sounds of leather rubbing leather, the soft tinkle of rein-chains and spur rowels, the occasional chukkering sound of horses clearing their nostrils, the night was totally quiet now. That rearward rumble of hooves was lost. Once, borne this far southward by an errant little breeze, they all heard several popping gunshots. But only that once; afterwards, with no more breeze to act as conductor of sounds from northward, there was nothing else to hear.

Laramie returned through the darkness in a standing trot. 'Nothin' as far as I could determine,' he reported to Buck. 'But the smell's still there where riders stirred up a dust some while back.' He swung in with the others saying, 'I heard cattle down there somewhere, but west, out in the valley.'

'Probably a bunch that got separated in the uproar,' mused Fred Naylor, and swore softly to himself evidently remembering with some chagrin how he'd been caught flat-footed.

The moon rose as the lot of them came to that break in the eastward mountains. It put a ghostly, wet paleness over everything. Buck studied each yard of that onward country until completely satisfied, then he said to Buff Evans, 'Good timing,' meaning the belated way the moon had arisen.

Buff said: 'Real good,' as he reined towards the pass. 'I never been down this far before; any place to hide the horses?'

Buck nodded. He said, 'Detail a couple of men as horse-holders. Tell them to lead the animals back up the pass out of bullet-range.' He paused, slowed to a halt and twisted. 'Fred; get down.' Naylor obeyed while around him all the other men also dismounted.

'Hey,' said Laramie Potter suddenly, in a sharp, breathless tone. 'Rider's comin'.'

CHAPTER EIGHT

The men were uncertain after Laramie's pronouncement. They did not at once relinquish their reins to the horse-holders moving among them.

Buck said to Fred Naylor: 'Give that owl call again; if they're our men, which I reckon they are, they'll perhaps answer.'

Naylor cupped both hands, gave out with that mournful sound, repeated it, then dropped his hand looking ahead.

At once those unseen riders halted. For an interval of time there was not a sound to be heard. Then a tentative voice called out:—

''That you, Fred?'

'Yeah. Who's that?'

'Curt and the others. Hey; you haven't seen Buck, have you?'

'He's right here beside me. Come on in, Curt.'

Buck turned, ran a look at the motionless men around him and nodded to them. 'Hand over your horses, fetch your carbines and come along.'

Curt Walker came stepping along cautiously until he recognised the others, then he swung his head. 'It's all right; come on in,' he called to the men with him.

Buck moved ahead a little scanning Walker's face. 'Anyone hurt?' he asked.

Walker wagged his head as he dismounted. 'Somebody said they saw Fred get it—but obviously that's not true.'

'My horse, not me,' growled Naylor, watching the others come into view and step down.

'Where's your Winchester, Fred?' a

76

newcomer asked.

Buff Evans made a rumbling chuckle and said, 'He lost it. When the shootin' commenced he got so scairt he run right out from under it.'

Naylor swore a rattling oath and other men also chuckled.

The horse-holders took every animal and started up the pass with them. Buck, standing in the rough centre of his men, counted noses. Everyone was accounted for except Burton Riddle and the men with him back at the camp site.

'Check your guns,' he directed, 'then head up the pass a short ways. Get behind the rocks up there, or trees, or anything you can find, and wait. I figured JG would be along by now but maybe old Burt put up more of a scrap than I figured on. Anyway, get under cover, keep quiet, and when you hear riders coming, don't do anything until I tell you to.'

The men began dispersing. Overhead, that lopsided old moon rode serenely upon its orbit casting pewter light downward. In the pass itself visibility was not particularly good, but out upon the dry-grass plain there was a diaphanous reflection of light which made it possible for the pothook men to see several hundred yards ahead.

Buck, standing in the centre of the pass's wide trail looking to see that all his men were out of sight, was approached by Fred Naylor.

77

'This ought to be about like shootin' fish in a rain-barrel,' said Naylor.

Buck nodded, cast a final look around, saw nothing which might reveal to oncoming horsemen that this was an ambuscade, and started towards an eroded stone needle on the north side. Fred followed him, got in behind the same rock and squatted down. Some night-roosting birds in a brush patch part way up the sidehill, disturbed by all the talk and noise, chirped drowsily, garrulously. A man rose up from behind a low stone, peered around, darted to a larger boulder and faded from sight behind it.

Moments passed, the hush lengthened, and from the trail's south side a man said plaintively: 'What the hell's keepin' 'em?' No one answered him.

Suddenly a wisp of darting movement appeared just beyond the pass. Buck saw it; so did nearly every other man. The sharp, quick sound of guns being cocked sounded from nearly two dozen vantage points. That man-shape dropped low and a voice hissed: 'They're comin'. I scouted out a ways an' heard 'em.'

Buck recognised that voice and hissed back. 'Laramie; if you're plumb tired of livin' do that stupid stunt once more.'

Potter murmured: 'Well; we had to know, didn't we?' and shunted out of sight among the boulders which lay upon both sides of the pass

78

leading out of the Devil's Punch Bowl.

Fred Naylor grumbled something under his breath and twisted around to have a view outward over the valley floor. Beside him also watching, still and silent, Buck stood easy, his carbine cradled in one arm, his hat back, his body leaning upon the rough-surfaced stone which shielded him.

Gradually a roiled sound came into the atmosphere; it steadily deepened, coming on, until it was the recognisable sound of many horsemen riding hurriedly all in a bunch.

Buck said nothing; he raised his carbine, took a rest with his free arm upon the stone spire, put the gun across it, and slowly snugged low over the gun-stock. Fred Naylor, still squatting, squared around also bringing his weapon to bear.

A man's rough voice sounded close to the pass's entrance and somewhere farther back another man answered garrulously saying that he was all right, that it had been just a lucky shot and didn't hurt much anyway.

Those oncoming sounds firmed up into shapes of men and horses. Buck watched them materialise out of the milky night. He let them swing in fairly close then he said to Fred Naylor: 'Steady, steady,' and squeezed off his first shot.

That explosion, bracketed as it was by both steep canyon walls, sounded howitzer-like in the dead night. Instantly other muzzles flamed outward too. Somewhere ahead a horse screamed and a man's bull-bass voice cried out as much in astonishment as in alarm. Only one full sentence was discernible before the gunfire over-rode everything else.

'They didn't run out, dammit all.'

Just that one high gush of words before all hell broke loose at the mouth of the pass leading out of the Devil's Punch Bowl, but it was enough for Buck, who not only heard it, but guessed at its implication. Someone among those JG night-riders, seeking a plausible reason for the absence of resistance on the part of Buck's men, had come up with the notion that the free-graze men had fled in panic from JG's savage attack.

Buck fired, levered up and fired again. He had a fierce little smile around his lips; JG was finding out just how wrong its premature judgement had been.

For almost a full minute there was no return-fire. The free-graze men had a field-day of it for that little length of time firing at frantically fleeing men, some afoot, others fighting their panicked animals in the midst of a hail of lead.

A whip-lash voice commanded the JG riders to come together, to charge the pass. That was when the return-fire came witheringly. Buck and Fred Naylor were driven low behind their shielding boulder with singing lead ricocheting around them and solidly striking stone in front of them.

For many seconds this pitched battle continued, but in the end it culminated in the only way it could, since the free-graze men were protected and JG was not.

'Break it off,' a man howled out upon the valley floor. 'Get clear of 'em, they're holed up in them gawdamned rocks yonder.'

Because this made sense, also because that devastating fire from Buck's cowboys never once diminished in volume or ferocity, JG's riders began withdrawing. For a while yet there was gunfire, but it atrophied as the moments passed until, down near the pass's entrance, Laramie Potter's reedy voice called out: 'Busted 'em fair an' square, boys. Knocked hell out'n 'em.'

Buck risked a look around his boulder. There was nothing moving as far as he could see, but there were a number of dark lumps beyond the pass, wholly still and silent. Because Laramie was still crowing, Buck sang out for silence. When it came every man in his hiding place heard the distant beat of running horses heading due west on across the valley.

'That,' pronounced Buck, moving out into the trail, 'is what I'd hoped to hear.' He swung around bawling out: 'Horse-holders; fetch the animals down here on the double!'

Fred Naylor stood up. He was reloading his saddle-gun. Percy Devlin and Buff Evans came trotting up. Behind them other men also came running. There was considerable gleeful talk as the pothook riders gathered where Buck stood. Only Fred Naylor remained at the rock; he was gazing steadily at Buck. After a little time he said dryly, 'Buck; you sound just like a damned army officer.'

Buck, checked by this comment, looked long at Naylor. He ruefully smiled. 'Habit I reckon,' he said. 'Sorry, Fred.'

Naylor walked forward from the rock saying, 'Oh, that's all right. Since you aren't one I don't mind. But durin' the war I got a craw-full o' hearin' officers yell orders when I knew as well as they did what had to be done.'

Buck, still affecting that contrite look, watched the horse-holders come down the pass. He turned finally to gaze steadily over at Naylor and say: 'All right, Fred; what's our next move?'

Naylor stopped. 'Why; head for camp as quick as we can, naturally,' he said.

Buck thinly smiled. The men looked from one to the other of them. 'That may be what we ought to do, Fred,' retorted Buck, 'but it's not what we're going to do.

'No? Then what?'

Buck waved a hand westerly. 'You heard JG run off in that direction, didn't you?'

'Sure; all of us did. What of it?'

'Well; if you'll think back, Fred, you'll remember that the only way out of this place is not along the west rims—but along the east rims.'

'There might be trails over the west mountains,' Naylor said, sounding uncertain about this and as though he did not believe it himself.

'There might be,' Buck shot right back. 'Let's assume there are. It'll take them the rest of the night to get across the valley. It'll take them half of tomorrow to climb to those rims, circle around the Punch Bowl an' get back over here on the east side. Then, it'll take them at least another two, three hours to get from here to Graeme's ranch.'

Naylor wasn't looking at Buck any longer; he was instead giving his scratched carbine butt a minute inspection. Buck waited briefly for him to speak; when it was apparent Naylor would not do so, he went on to conclude what he had in mind.

'We out-manoeuvred them here at the pass, and now we're going to out-manoeuvre them again,' he told the pothook riders standing near and listening. 'We're not going back to camp at all. Old Burt and the men with him are safe enough; JG won't hit them again tonight.' He took the reins Buff Evans held out to him, turned, toed in and rose up to settle over leather. 'We're going on over to JG and repay this social call. Get mounted, boys, it's quite a ways from here.'

Laramie Potter, in the act of whittling a

corner off his chewing plug with a wicked-looking Mexican boot-knife, looked up and around at Buck. He had frank admiration showing in his face.

'Of course,' he stated to the other riders. 'Now why didn't I think o' that.'

'Because,' growled Fred Naylor, speaking at last as he went to his horse, 'you wasn't no blamed officer in the war, that's why. Well; don't just stand there—get aboard, you heard what Cap'n Handley said.'

Buff Evans came hoofing it in from beyond the pass. He halted beside Buck to say: 'If we hurt any of 'em the others must've packed 'em off. There are four dead horses out there but no men.' He caught the reins someone tossed him. He mounted and reined over beside Buck to finish with: 'An' you wouldn't believe it, but every blamed one o' those dead horses has a big JG brand on his hip as plain as day.'

Laramie Potter, who had heard this, pouched his cud of tobacco, artfully expectorated, and wagged his head. 'Just can't be sure who your friends are any more, can you?' he said.

They clattered up the pass and broke out on to the yonder plains under a scudding cloud that momentarily hid the moon. Ahead of them the land ran on in a gently sloping way for a mile, then lifted again, and fell again, completing its undulating pattern.

They crossed through clumps of second-growth trees and came upon a bone-dry creek which echoed their passing in a rattling way. After the second mile Buck sent Buff Evans and Curt Walker on ahead to scout; it was, he told Fred, who was behind him on the same horse again, a needless precaution, but one which he always observed out of habit.

Naylor, properly chastened after their discussion back at the pass, said nothing; just concentrated upon maintaining his balance, not the easiest thing to do under the circumstances.

A rider loped up beside Naylor and held out a Winchester. 'Buff said to give you this; he found it beyond the pass. He wants his carbine back.'

This exchange was made, the rider dropped back again, and Fred bucketed along behind Buck, balancing the carbine over his lap.

That scudding cloud passed along, the moon popped out coating the world with its melancholy light again, and somewhere far ahead a horse whistled, bringing Buck and his pothook riders down to a cautious walk.

CHAPTER NINE

Evans and Walker returned. They had encountered a band of brood-mares and a big palomino stud-horse, they reported, but beyond that—nothing.

'You didn't go far enough,' said Buck. 'JG's on ahead. But that's all right—come on.'

They continued forward, but slowly now. The only talk was made by Naylor who told Buff Evans the least he could have done out there was to rope one of those horses so Fred wouldn't have to ride double. Buff's reply to this was caustic: 'Every one of 'em's heavy with foal, but if you don't mind ridin' old bred mares with your legs stickin' straight out like match-sticks, why I reckon we can still get you one of those mares.'

Naylor said no more.

Buck spotted JG's dark buildings hull-down on the dark horizon before the others did. He stopped to consider them thinking that there should have been lights, if not at the main house then at least at the bunkhouse.

From behind him Fred Naylor, also squinting ahead, said, 'Pretty dark over there. Maybe no one's to home.'

Buck made no comment. He led out another two hundred yards, halted and swung down. There would be someone at the ranch, he was certain of that.

Curt Walker and Perc Devlin ambled up. Pere said, 'It smells like a trap to me.'

Buck, thinking along the same lines, faintly nodded. 'I'll scout ahead,' he told the men closest him. 'You boys stay quiet.'

JG's ranch buildings were made of peeled

logs. They were square, massive, and enduring. The main house sat some little distance from a huge barn, a roomy bunkhouse, a combination smithy and saddle-house, and several smaller buildings. There was not a sound, a light, or a sign of movement anywhere around them.

Buck, leaving his Winchester with his horse, had no difficulty getting up to the edge of JG's quiet yard. He paused near some pole-corrals, leaned there peering ahead for several minutes, then set a course for the bunkhouse. If there was anyone at JG they'd be at either the main residence or the bunkhouse.

There was a feeling to the atmosphere around JG which Buck could not quite pin down; it appeared to be part foreboding, part lethal tension, and part deadliness. By the time he was in behind a little tool shed that feeling was so strong he halted and remained where he was for a long time, acutely conscious of it.

He heard a man clear his throat.

That was it; JG was not abed nor was the ranch abandoned. Somewhere ahead were motionless watchers.

Buck pressed closer into the gloom around his little shed blocking in squares of yard, examining each of these areas minutely. It took a long time to do this and he found no shadows, no silhouettes, no shifting outlines of men although he was sure now there were men around him.

He drew back, studied his inward route, then undertook a careful withdrawal. For a half-hour he was between those hidden men and his pothook riders passing through a dead-silent world of moon-dappled night. Where he ultimately encountered his riders again Percy Devlin and Laramie Potter, who were both equally tall, lean, and lethal, saw him first and stepped out to intercept him.

Percy said, 'Sure as hell old Jethro an' his girl wasn't with them night-riders, was they, Buck; then how come the ranch to be deserted?'

'It's not deserted,' replied Handley, moving in among the men. 'I don't know who's planning for JG but I'll tell you this—he's no novice. I figured, after scattering those attackers, we'd have a clean run at JG.'

'And,' asked Art Waters, 'don't we have a clear run?'

Buck shook his head. 'Maybe they figured some of us would get away from the fight in the valley and come over here to raise a little hell of our own. At any rate, there are men up there among those buildings, waiting.'

'Men,' said a cowboy quizzically. 'How? Hell; that bunch we busted at the pass numbered, from the looks of their gun-flashes, to be at least twenty—which was the number old Graeme had with him yesterday.'

'I know,' Buck replied. 'I wondered about that too. The only thing I can come up with is

88

that more of the gunmen Graeme said he was hiring, have come up a day early.'

'That's likely all right,' growled Fred Naylor. 'Them kind are hungry; they can smell a job like a buzzard smells carrion.' He wrinkled his forehead at Buck. 'But how come 'em to be waitin' for us? There's something wrong here, Buck, I can feel it. They're out-guessin' us somehow.'

Buck frowned. He put himself in Jethro Graeme's place and tried thinking as a cold rational old cowman would think. Graeme, planning for the worst, would without doubt take every precaution to protect his ranch. He would not believe his attackers would fail down in the valley, yet he would prepare for this possibility all the same. That had to be it.

Granting that this was so, then, Buck now had to consider how old Jethro could be beaten at his own game. He and his pothook men had plenty of time; those JG night-riders would not come up behind them until long after sun-up, but what he wished he now knew was just how many men were standing guard up there among the JG buildings.

'Listen to me a minute,' spoke up Laramie Potter. 'Perc an' I can slip up there and catch us one of them fellers maybe, an' . . .'

'Maybe,' said Fred Naylor dourly. 'Laramie; I've been huntin' with you an' seen you stumble over your own feet. I'll go. I'll sneak up there and catch us one of them night-ridin' whelps.'

Buck distantly heard this discussion while making his decision. He spoke out right after Naylor finished, saying, 'Graeme's foreman said the old man was going to have fifty riders to oppose us with. All right, we scattered at least twenty men down at the pass. Now, if all the other gunmen Graeme hired rode in today, which isn't very likely, then he'll still only have another twenty-five or thirty at the ranch. Those aren't bad odds, boys, when you consider that we've got the darkness on our side. But I don't think he'll have that many, and furthermore I don't think, even if he has, that every one of those fellers is standin' guard. So—we all go forward. All but the horse-holders.'

Naylor nodded at this logic. 'Take carbines?' he asked.

'No carbines. They reflect light. Besides, at close distance we won't need them.'

The same men who cared for their saddlestock at the pass again gathered the horses as their companions started onward.

Buck led out. Not a sound was made all the way to JG's dark buildings. Buck led them in behind the pole-corrals where shadow-patterns in the moonlight effectively camouflaged every man. He was studying the yonder main house when a set of fingers fell lightly upon his arm. He turned to find Fred Naylor scarcely breathing at his side, and looking ahead and to their right, over where the bunkhouse stood.

'Watch,' Naylor whispered, and did not elaborate on this.

All of them swung their attention towards the bunkhouse. It was not a very long wait; the glowing red tip of a cigarette flared where a smoker inhaled, then it paled out to a sullen faint red as the man let his hand drop.

'Against the bunkhouse wall,' said Buck.

'Can you make him out? I can't,' stated Naylor.

'Never mind that.' Buck swung, found Buff Evans directly behind him and said, 'Keep everyone here, Buff. Don't make a sound. Fred and I'll go up there.'

Evans nodded; the other men pushed up closer to watch, and Buck, brushing Naylor's arm with his fingers, started around the corrals southward.

The distance to be covered was perhaps three hundred feet. Where that cigarette occasionally glowed it was not possible to make out the man smoking it because of deep darkness along that side of the log bunkhouse. This, though, worked both ways, for as soon as Buck and Fred Naylor were into the same dark square of blackness, that unseen man could not make them out either, unless they moved, which they did not do once they were close enough to discern the slope of masculine shoulders, the graceful curve of a tilted-back hat, and the slouched position of this stranger leaning there with a Winchester resting beside him against logs.

Buck twisted to shoot Fred a look. They were less than a hundred feet from the sentinel. Naylor dropped his head, put his lips to Buck's ear and said: 'Probably a dozen more in the bunkhouse. One sound and we're in bad trouble.'

Buck nodded, drew away, carefully drew his handgun and, waiting for the sentry to shift a little, to swing his bored gaze eastward, took a half dozen onward steps which brought him still closer in the night. He paused, fixing his whole attention upon that guard's lazily-moving head, then went onward again. In this fashion, although it took him nearly fifteen minutes to accomplish it, he ultimately got to the corner of the log house.

He stood steady here looking back at the spot where he'd left Naylor. Fred was nowhere to be seen. A full sixty seconds passed; Buck looked around the roughwood corner, saw his guard remove his hat, scratch, put the hat back on, and prodigiously yawn. He stepped around the building at the precise moment the guard turned, one hand going out to take up the Winchester. The guard saw Buck move; saw his gun in the darkness and saw his flinty face. He froze, his reaching hand motionless in mid-air.

Buck took several closer steps. He said nothing at all and for a moment those two men stared at one another scarcely breathing. The sentinel finally squared his shoulders drawing up erect. He let his reaching arm fall to his side. He was a heavy-shouldered man, narrow-hipped and bow-legged. His face was flat with coarse features. The eyes, hatbrim-shadowed, were very pale and very still; this man was a killer.

Buck motioned gently. The guard stepped away from that propped Winchester. He was co-operating but he never took his eyes off his captor. He also still had a holstered six-gun.

Buck caught up the carbine, pressed flat against the log wall and motioned for the sentry to pass westerly in front of him. Again the man obeyed. As he went by, though, he measured Handley with a hard look; he was captured but his look said very plainly that he was not beaten.

Fred Naylor stepped from behind the bunkhouse. He and the prisoner exchanged a look. Naylor put up a hand, roughly shoved the guard, and fell in behind him driving him along towards the corral.

The three of them got back where the pothook men waited. At once the prisoner was totally disarmed, surrounded by hard-faced riders, and the last of his defiance wilted. He was not afraid but he was cognizant that escape, resistance, or even crying out an alarm, were no longer to be thought of. He relaxed, gave the pothook men stare for stare, and after a while he shrugged, leaned upon corral poles and said quietly, evenly: 'All right, fellers, you got me—now what?'

Buck stepped up close. 'How many men are stationed around the yard?'

'Nine. The old man put 'em out. Me, I just got in this afternoon. I was dog-tired or you'd never have got up on me like that.'

'How many in the bunkhouse?'

'Six.'

'Fifteen all told?'

The gunman nodded, appraising Buck.

'We want them. All of them.'

The gunman's brows hiked upwards, his cold eyes widened. 'Want 'em? Want 'em for what, mister?'

'For the same thing we wanted you for—prisoners.'

'Is that so? An' just how'n hell do you aim to get 'em?'

Short, burly Buff Evans pushed up very close to the prisoner. 'You're kind of smart, aren't you?' he said, his face alight with the will to fight. 'I'm a head shorter'n you; how about takin' a swing at me?'

The prisoner looked hard at Buff, then wagged his head. 'Don't care for the odds,' he mumbled. Then said, 'Maybe another time.'

'Right damned now,' snarled Evans, 'unless you give some respectful answers.'

The larger man looked over at Buck. He nodded, still looking unafraid, but showing something like respect or deference in his fresh glance. 'All right, mister; we'll do it your way. For now, at least.'

Buck put a glance upon Evans. The burly, fight-scarred short man shuffled back into the crowd of surrounding cowboys.

'The six in the bunkhouse we can take easy enough,' said Buck to the captive. 'It's the other nine I'm thinking about.'

No one said anything. Perc Devlin spat out a cud of tobacco, peered around into the night, then leaned upon a corral post. Fred Naylor said, 'How about some kind of a ruse, Buck?'

Laramie Potter snorted. 'Like what?' he demanded. 'Buck; you said we got plenty o' time to do this. Well then; all we got to do is get inside the JG cook-shack, wait for breakfast, an' take the lot of 'em as they troop in to fill out the slack in their bellies.' Laramie smiled. 'I an' some other fellers once captured a whole danged platoon of blue-belly soljers like that in the war. Want to try it?'

Buck faintly smiled. 'We'll try it,' he assented. 'One of you gag and bind our friend here.'

CHAPTER TEN

Gaining entrance to the JG cookhouse took time. For one thing, the guards throughout the yard had first to be located in order to be avoided. This took until midnight. Secondly, for fifteen heavily armed men, booted and spurred, to stealthily make their way to the cook-shack could not be done swiftly.

These things were ultimately accomplished but it was close to three o'clock in the morning before they were, then an unexpected crisis developed. No sooner had the last pothook rider gotten into that long, dark room with its scarred table, its long benches and its squeaky floor, than through the wall came the cough and groan of JG's cook who slept in a lean-to off the dining-room. Buck's men heard him roll over, cough again, then hit the floor in stockinged feet.

'The *cosinero*,' breathed Buck. 'Pass the word—not a sound.'

Among them only two men carried watches. Both at once took out their time-pieces, opened each case and peered closely at the spidery little black hands. Laramie Potter, not one of those who had a watch, nevertheless craned over the shoulder of a man who did have, and afterwards bent far over to whisper to Buck.

'Kind of early for a ranch cook to be rollin' out. It's not quite three o'clock.'

This observation, true though it was, could just as easily been left unsaid, for a rumpled head popped through a little door, JG's cook emerged, paused to stretch, yawn, vigorously scratch his belly and let off a loud sigh. He afterwards went stocking-footedly out into the long room bound for a large iron cook-stove across the way. He hadn't progressed quite ten feet when a six-gun-muzzle brought him to a jarred halt. The weapon was in Laramie Potter's fist; it had been roughly jammed into the cook's back.

'Not a sound,' husked Laramie. 'Not one damned peep or you'll never work up another batch of biscuits.'

Laramie steered the thoroughly astonished cook over in front of Buck. The man's eyes bulged wide at sight of so many blurred shadows converging upon him. He looked left, he looked right, then he halted and put his startled face towards Handley.

'What the hell,' he breathed.

'Up kind of early, aren't you?' Buck said mildly. 'What's the occasion; someone's birthday?'

The cook's face gradually lost its startled expression. He squinted upwards. 'You're that free-grazer,' he exclaimed. 'Mister Graeme'll have a fit when he finds you here.'

'He isn't going to find me, pardner. Answer

my question; how come you're up so early?'

'Well,' said the cook, and stopped to cast a slow look at the dark ring of armed men around him. 'King Lewis tol' me to make some coffee and fried meat.'

'This early?' persisted Buck.

'Well . . .'

'Oh hell,' grumbled Laramie, who still had his gun in the cook's back. 'Let's knock him over the head an' . . .'

'No,' the cook said swiftly. 'I'll tell you. King went down to the Devil's Punch Bowl with the boys. He said he'd be back about four, no later, and he wanted breakfast then.'

Buck nodded, long since having concluded this was the reason for the cook's early rising. 'What about the men guarding the yard an' the ones in the bunkhouse; were they going to eat at the same time?'

'Yes.'

'Why?'

'Ahh; what d'you mean—"why"? They got to eat, don't they? I mean, breakfast is . . .'

Laramie rammed his gun so hard into the cook's back the man's words were bitten off and lost in a loud gasp of agony. Laramie said nothing; neither did any of the other men. Like Buck, they were all bleakly staring.

The cook recovered his voice and blurted: 'King said for me to roust 'em all up an' have 'em ready to eat as soon as he got back.'

Buck said simply: 'Why?' In that same mild

tone. By now though, the cook was sufficiently intimidated not to be deceived by that soft mildness. He answered at once, pushing his words all together in fright.

'Because when the whole crew'd be together he figured to go back to the Punch Bowl and—and—round up all your critters an' bust 'em out o' the valley up into the forests where they'd likely not be found again for maybe a year or so.'

'I see,' stated Buck. 'And a year from now he figured we'd be either dead or gone out of the country, which would make a pretty handsome nest-egg for whoever rounded up our cattle and sold 'em. 'That it?'

'Well; he never said that, mister.'

Fred Naylor pushed up close to the cook. Fred, when he wished to, could look murderous; he used that expression now; he stared until the cook blinked, looked away, and blinked some more, then Fred said: 'I'll go with you; we'll fetch back JG's gunhands together.'

Laramie objected to this at once. 'What're you thinkin' of,' he growled. 'They'll know you.'

'How?' challenged Naylor. 'How will they? Hell; gunmen been ridin' in here for the last twenty-four hours that're even strangers to each other. How'll they know I'm not another one like the others?'

Buff Evans rumbled agreement with this; so

99

did most of the other fifteen men. Even Buck nodded, so Potter subsided, turning his attention back to the thoroughly shaken, stocking-footed, rumple-haired JG cook. He withdrew his pistol from this man's back, eased off the dog and holstered the gun. He put a big, rough hand upon the cook's shoulder, turned him around and lowered his face until it was inches away.

'Pardner,' he growled, 'you so much as raise an eyebrow to sound a warning, and I'll carve your heart out an' feed it to the crows.'

Buck, his face shadowed in soft darkness, could not entirely repress a smile over the cook's reaction to this threat; to the cumulative threat of all the hostile men around him.

He said, 'Laramie, you tag along with Fred and our prisoner here. And keep that Mex boot-knife you carry right handy just in case. The rest of you go over along the front wall. Keep a lookout through the windows into the yard. If anything breaks, shoot and shoot straight. Otherwise just stand easy until the gunhands walk in here.' When Buck finished speaking he crossed to a lamp, removed the mantle, turned up the wick and prepared to make a light.

Percy Devlin protested about having light in the room but Buck ignored him to say, 'Go on, Fred. You and Laramie get moving. We'll be waiting.' He made no move to light the lamp until those three had passed out into the darkness closing the door after themselves. After that, he said to Perc Devlin: 'Find a couple more of these lights. Fetch them over here. This light is going to help us, not hinder us. You'll see.'

Perc stalked around the big room until he located several more lamps. These he took over to Buck; he watched as they were lighted, flooding that gaunt old room with a brightness the other men moved away from.

'Bring 'em along,' ordered Buck.

He and Devlin placed the lamps directly in front of the cook-shack doorway, upon benches there. Devlin's expression cleared. 'I get it,' he said. 'Anyone comin' through that door gets light plumb in the eyes. Right?'

'Right. And if these hirelings of old Graeme's feel like making a play, we'll see it coming. Get over by the door with the others, Perc.'

Buck watched his riders, saw that they thoroughly understood what they were to do, and left them to enter the cook's lean-to room off the dining-room. Here, he found a long-barrelled shotgun in a corner, a belted six-gun dangling over the back of a chair, which he unloaded, and the meagre effects of a cow-camp cook. When he returned to the main hall he was carrying that shotgun over one arm. Art Waters saw him halt on across the room opposite the doorway with the big table in front of him, and said: 'Be careful with that blessed thing. It may be long-barrelled but that shot'll still scatter like rice.'

Buck had no time to comment on this. Curt Walker, standing west of the doorway with four other bunched-up riders, called softly: 'Here come the first of 'em. They were in the bunkhouse.' Curt paused to chuckle. 'Six of 'em, an' I'll be damned if two of 'em haven't got their shell-belts slung over their shoulders, not even puttin' them on. Now that's what I call being sleepy.'

'No shooting,' ordered Buck. 'No shooting or loud talk unless they start it. Curt; the second every last one of them is inside, close the door. The rest of you throw down on 'em; cock your guns behind 'em. Funny thing about a gun being cocked—the bravest men on earth suddenly go limp all over at that little sound.'

The others, watching Curt Walker, saw him straighten up a little, saw him draw his six-gun and swing so that he was facing the door. Every man of them took a cue from this; the only sound in the cookhouse now was the rough whisper of steel barrels sliding upwards out of leather holsters.

The door opened. A youngish man stepped through, paused to look in a puzzled way at those lined-up lanterns directly ahead of him on the benches. Five others pushed in. One of them grumbled: 'Move; what you stoppin' there for?'

Walker pushed the door closed. Fifteen men behind those light-blinded men cocked their guns. Not one of those six gunmen moved; they were like statues. Only their eyes showed anything; they grew widely round and disbelieving. Directly ahead of them, behind the light and across the big table, Buck Handley cocked his shotgun; cocked both barrels and said: 'Curt; Art; Perc; disarm them.'

This was done readily and still those six gunmen did not move. Buck stepped up, put the shotgun upon the table and examined his captives. They were all young men excepting one; he was not actually old in years but dissipation and a hard life had given his face a look of age. To this man Buck said: 'Not a sound. Move off to the right. Keep your hands in plain sight and when your friends walk in here don't open your mouths. Now move!'

It was a painless triumph; the six men moved, took position directly in front of six free-graze riders and except for looking gradually outraged and venomous, they were still and silent.

Buck picked up the shotgun, stepped back against the far wall again, uncocked the weapon and resumed his waiting stance.

The second wait was longer and Curt Walker, keeping his vigil, fidgeted, an indication of uneasiness which transmitted itself to nearly every other free-graze man in

103

the room. The captives turned easy after some time had passed. They craned for looks around at their captors, at each other, and ahead across the room where Buck stood, pivotal figure in all this. The shotgun in his hands more than anything else kept any of those six men from getting any very high hopes.

'More coming,' said Walker softly. 'Too dark to make 'em out good but it looks like quite a bunch.' He turned away from the window, raised his gun and crouched a little where he faced the door.

Tension was in the room now, thick enough to cut with a knife. Buck ran a quick look around; he felt the pre-dawn chill which was creeping into the room, saw that his men were feeling this too, or if not the chill of dawn then at least some kind of a chill.

The free-graze men standing close behind their six prisoners, emulated Buff Evans. Buff, paying less heed to the doorway than to the man in front of him, eased a gun-barrel into his particular prisoner's back. There was no mistaking this silent warning. All six captives froze in their boots.

The door swung open and men trooped inside. As before, the first few halted to stare perplexedly at those lined-up lamps. Behind them other men spread out pushing around them farther into the cook-house. Someone let off an oath, saying: 'Why in hell ain't the stove lit? It's cold outside an' in here too.'

That was the last casual remark any of them made. Pushing in from the rear were Fred Naylor and lank Laramie Potter. Both had their guns out and now they cocked them. Buck at the same time recocked both his shotgun barrels.

'Freeze,' ordered Buck, those twin barrels pointing dead-ahead. 'Don't make a move any of you.'

Astonishment as much as those cocking guns held the newcomers completely still and staring. Potter and Naylor let no time for second thoughts pass; they moved in to begin stripping away holstered six-guns at once. Curt, Buff, Percy Devlin and others stepped forward to also do this. Before the JG gunhands recovered they were unarmed.

Buck counted them. 'Fourteen,' he said. 'Fifteen counting tousle-head here.' He meant the cook, who was looking at the shotgun in Buck's hands with recognition upon his face. 'With the one we left hog-tied over at the corral that should be all of them.' He gazed at the cook looking for confirmation of this, but none was forthcoming until Laramie, moving swiftly, caught the smaller man in a hard grip and shook him. Then the cook began to nod vigorously.

'That's right,' he croaked, still in Potter's grasp. 'Fifteen is all there is on the ranch—so far. King Lewis's got the others with . . .'

Buck cut across this gush of words.

105

'Laramie; you and Fred make sure it's safe to head out of here with our prisoners.'

'How about horses?' asked Potter.

'They can walk. It's only about seven miles to our camp. Go have a look around.'

CHAPTER ELEVEN

The simplest part of the entire night's work was leaving Jethro Graeme's ranch. Because there was no flurry of men mounting horses, no steel-shod hooves to rattle over the summer-hardened ranchyard, this withdrawal was accomplished in near silence.

The pothook riders herded their dour captives along until, near where they'd left their animals, Buck had them halt until Fred Naylor went ahead, told the horseholders what had happened, and brought their mounts to them. After that they rode along behind their captives with the overhead vault of heaven turning softly blue over in the hazy east. Dawn did not come entirely, though, until they were trooping down the pass into the Devil's Punch Bowl. Then it did, softly pink and endlessly hushed.

For those four miles of semi-darkness none of the prisoners had spoken. Now one of them did. He was a large, beefy man who stumped along as though his feet hurt. He turned to

Buck and said, 'How much farther; I'm about to give out. This here walkin' stuff is for squaw-Injuns an' fools.'

'Another three, four miles,' answered Buck. 'What's your name, feller?'

'To you it's Smith,' came back the growled reply.

'How much did Jethro Graeme agree to pay you, Mister Smith, for bushwhackin' us?'

Smith scowled darkly. 'Nothin' was said about bushwhackin',' he exclaimed. 'I don't know about the others but I was hired to protect JG against free-grazers.' He squinted upwards. 'If you're a free-grazer, mister, you're the smartest one I ever run across—or the luckiest.'

'How much?' repeated Buck.

'Seventy-five a month and found—plus ammunition.' Smith paced along with the other gunmen for a little ways, then he said bitterly: 'An' if I knew walkin' was included I wouldn't have taken the consarned job for twice that.'

Several pothook men laughed; even some of the other gunmen smiled at this, and at the obviously sincere and outraged expression of the man who had said it.

They were moving slowly northward up the valley when over a distant saw-toothed ridge the sun jumped up. Feeling the instantaneous heat which now came down into the valley, Buck twisted, caught Art Water's eye, and said, 'Sashay on ahead, find Burton, tell him we're bringin' company for breakfast, and help him set the camp to rights again.'

Waters departed in a long lope. As he spurred away Curt Walker edged over beside Buck. 'Might not be a bad idea if one or two of us sort of loped out a ways an' looked over the cattle. Haven't any of us seen if there was any damage since those night-riders hit us.'

Buck agreed, saying, 'Take whoever you want and go have a look. Also, Curt, while you're over on the west side, look around for tracks where King Lewis and those other JG men went. Be careful though; don't take any chances.'

Walker also left. He took for companion a man who had been slouching along twanging on a Jew's harp. This second cowboy's departure inspired Laramie Potter to say dryly: 'If he hadn't gone off with Curt I was plannin' on shootin' him for that noise he's got the guts to call music.'

One of their prisoners suddenly halted, planted both hands on his hips and glared up at the pothook riders. 'Not another lousy step,' this man exclaimed, 'until I get a drink of water.'

None of the horsemen had a canteen. Buck, considering the obdurate man, seeing for the first time the condition of his eyes, his face, said quietly, 'Mister; if you went on a spree yesterday and have a fire inside you today—

108

don't blame anyone but yourself. If we had any water you could have it but we don't have, and we're a half mile west of the river, so you just hike along there and shut up.'

The gunman glared at Buck. To one side of him Percy Devlin unbuttoned the romal of his braided reins, gripped this quirt-like appendage in one big hand and began reining his horse inward towards the stubborn man. Off to one side the big, beefy man who called himself Smith, said to the obdurate one: 'Get going; you want all of us to stand out here in the lousy sun while you make a play with a busted flush? Hey, you on the horse.' Smith was addressing Devlin. 'Leave him alone; he'll go along.' Percy checked himself. Smith made a big sigh, pushed aside the gunmen nearest him and started forward with his mincing, rolling gait, towards the man who'd demanded water. His purpose was plain enough and the other gunman, slight of build, unmarred by bar-room brawls as was Smith, put a swift look at that big man bearing down upon him, then started forward sullenly, saying over one shoulder. 'Who's side you on anyway?'

'My own,' growled Smith. 'At least until we get to shade an' a place where I can sit down and shed these damned boots. Now keep movin'.'

Percy exchanged an amused look with Buck, reined back to the riding column beside their captives, and went along humming a little tune.

An hour later, where the San Juan made one of its westerly curvings, they came to water and shade. Everyone rushed ahead to drink and Buck had the pothook men water the horses downstream. For some little time no one volunteered to leave the coolness of the riverbank with its willows and its lulling, soft-lapping sounds. Out away from the river that breathless heat was piling up over the valley bringing on its gelatin layers of quivering haze again.

Where Buck stood with five or six of his men, the gunman called Smith walked over, sat down upon a boulder and proceeded to remove both boots and gaze forlornly at his feet.

'Boiled,' he announced. 'Boiled to a pulp with all the walkin' in this cussed sunshine.' He looked up, his dark eyes accusing. 'You said it wasn't much farther,' he said to Buck. 'Maybe to you—on a horse—farther don't mean the same thing it does to me on these boiled feet.'

Laramie Potter smiled raffishly. ' 'Tell you what, Smith; to rest your feet I'll carry the boots an' you can finish the hike barefooted.'

Percy Devlin, chewing a cud of tobacco, laughed aloud. Men turned to look over where Smith was sitting, considering Laramie from baleful eyes.

'You skinny excuse for a man,' rumbled Smith, pushing upright off his rock and glaring. 'Gun or no gun I got a notion to bust your smart-alec neck for you.'

'Barefooted?' asked Devlin, moving in a little closer. 'Barefooted on this hot sand?'

'Mister,' said Buck, crookedly smiling, 'put your boots back on and shut up.' He and Smith exchanged a long look. Smith sat down, pulled on his boots and sat a moment gazing unhappily at them before he stood up.

'You know,' he said conversationally to Buck, 'I didn't care one way or the other about JG's war with you free-grazers—until you made me walk like this. Now I'm startin' to take a real dislike to you boys.' Smith spat aside, wiped his chin and glared. 'I met King Lewis once, in a little trail-town. He ain't exactly what you'd call a friend of mine, but if he was here right now I think him an' me could clean out the lot of you—just us two.'

Fred Naylor snorted at this. 'You're a mighty poor judge of men,' he told Smith. 'Lewis already tried that—and he didn't get past Buck here.'

'Fact is,' piped up Laramie Potter, 'when Buck got through with him he was bleedin' like a stuck hog and had to be carried off by his JG riders.' Laramie cocked his head, considered the way Smith was studying Buckley, and concluded with: 'You still think the two of you could do it?'

Smith didn't answer; he turned, ran a look over where the other prisoners were sitting in

111

deep shade listening to this exchange, and said a savage word.

When they left the river Buck led out. A quarter-mile onward he spotted Art Waters loping towards him from the north. He spurred ahead to a meeting and slowed when Waters came up alongside.

'Burt's got camp re-established,' Waters reported. 'Neither he nor the fellers with him even got scratched last night when JG hit the camp.'

'Have they brought the wagons together again?' Buck asked, looking ahead through the thickening heat-haze for sight of the wagon-camp.

'Yeah. They got everything set to rights again. But old Burt's madder'n a hornet. He was worried too, when the rest of us didn't come back.' Waters ruefully shook his head. 'For a bad cook Burt's sure a good swearer,' he said. 'When I told him what we'd done an' that we were fetchin' those JG gunhands along for breakfast, the air just plain turned blue with his cussin'.'

'Go on back and give him a hand,' ordered Buck. 'He'll be able to use it. Maybe that'll sort of simmer him down a little.'

Waters' expression plainly said that he doubted this very much, but he wheeled around and loped off northward again.

When the wagon-camp finally hove into view a pothook man back near the end of the line raised a high cry. Every head turned in his direction. He was pointing south-westerly where two horsemen were coming up in a steady hard trot. It was Curt Walker and the cowboy he'd taken with him out to look at the pothook cattle.

Buck halted, motioned for the others to keep on going, and let Walker whip in beside him. The heat was by now fiercely unpleasant to man and beast. As Buck and Walker rode along the cowboy with the Jew's harp pushed ahead to join the main party of men; the back of his shirt was dark with perspiration.

' 'Cattle look all right,' Walker told Buck. 'Leastways as far as we went there didn't appear to be no dead ones. We saw some though that looked like they were the critters JG ran over the camp.'

'Any hurt ones?'

'Naw; a few with scratches, a few gimpy-footed, but they're all eatin' good and lookin' sassy.'

'How about Lewis's tracks?'

'It was about like you figured last night. Him an' them other JG boys went across the valley straight as an arrow. We didn't track 'em plumb up into the rocks over there—wasn't any need as far as I could see—but that's sure enough where they went. Right up into the danged rimrocks over there.' Walker paused to fling water off his chin, then he said, 'But we found another dead horse, which means

113

Lewis's men'll be packin' a lot of riders double, and that'll slow 'em even more. So maybe they won't get back to JG as fast as you figured, Buck.'

'I sure feel bad about that,' said Buck dryly, and booted out his horse. 'Come on; let's get up to camp while there's still some coffee left.'

When Art Waters had reported that Burton Riddle was angry he had not over-emphasised a condition which Buck saw from several hundred feet out, before he and Curt Walker rode on into camp. Burt had food ready, but he also had a considerable store of invective ready.

He was berating the pothook men only slightly less than their tired, sweaty, and glum prisoners. He dished up stew, coffee, and dried prunes with impartiality. With each helping too, regardless of who the recipient was, he also served up a scathing denunciation, topped off with the most dire and grisly prophecies of the end every man within his sight was inevitably going to come to.

Buck's appearance caused Burt to pause, but not for long, then the swearing commenced all over again. The JG gunman called Smith looked admiringly at Riddle, for this blasphemous moment forgetting his steaming feet.

Buck let the tirade run on for a time, then he crossed over, tapped the camp-cook on the shoulder from behind and when Riddle hopped around on his game leg to see who had the audacity to accost him, Buck put up a finger over his lips, said nothing at all, and stood there steadily staring until Riddle's hoarse voice dwindled to a whisper. Then Buck stepped around to the coffee pot, filled a tin mug, sipped for a moment and smiled at his cook. Old Riddle's flashing eyes mellowed a little.

'Mighty fine coffee,' said Buck in that mild way of his. He turned to survey the eating men around him upon the ground, more than three dozen of them. 'How about it, boys, anyone ever taste finer coffee or eat a better meal?'

No one had; at least the eight or ten men who opened up verbally in reply to this said they never had. It was JG's dour, rough-looking Smith who completed the smoothing of Burton Riddle's ruffled feathers, though.

'The coffee's hot an' the food's welcome,' he said, still gazing up at Burt. 'But it's his powerful language that plumb overwhelms me. Tell me, cookie, where in the wide world did you learn to cuss like that? It's a real pleasure to hear a man do that who knows how. I take my hat off to you.'

Burton Riddle blinked suspiciously at Smith until he saw the genuine admiration in the raffish gunfighter's face. He then hobbled to the fire, took up the coffee pot, picked his way among the other squatting men and said, 'Care for some more coffee, stranger? A little more hash maybe, or another handful of them dried prunes?'

Smith held up his cup, watched Riddle fill it, nodded his thanks and threw a broad wink over at Buck. 'You got to know how to handle men,' he said aloud. 'You got to know how to appreciate 'em.'

Buck smiled; he found himself liking the big, tough JG gunman in spite of himself. He winked back.

CHAPTER TWELVE

After every man had been fed several volunteered to ride out to the herd. Buck accepted this offer, yet because the day was approaching that time when he thought Lewis and more JG riders might be once more appearing in the valley, he sent out two bands of riders, one under leadership of Laramie Potter, the other under burly Buff Evans.

Four men were set to watching the prisoners, who needed very little watching; after that arduous hike, the big meal and the lassitude which followed both, these men crawled under wagons, under the texas-shelters, and almost immediately fell into a tired sleep. The man calling himself Smith was the last to seek rest; stepping gingerly in his stocking feet, carrying both boots in one great, scarred fist, he minced over where Buck was talking with Burton Riddle and Perc Devlin, eased into the shade there and waited until Buck turned towards him.

'I'll tell you how it is with me, Mister Handley,' he said. 'I'm not against free-grazers. I'm not against anythin' really, exceptin' horse-mules and bitin' dogs. Now, for my regular pay I'd be willin' to . . .'

'Thanks,' cut in Buck dryly. 'I don't need you. You're probably a good gunhand. Old Graeme wouldn't have hired you otherwise. But I don't hire gunfighters.'

Smith puckered up his face until both dark eyes were hidden in pouches of dark flesh. 'Maybe you'd better commence hirin' 'em,' he said evenly. 'I only got to JG yesterday afternoon late, but I can tell you this much—King Lewis and old Jethro Graeme make an unbeatable team—for average cowboys to tangle with.'

Lanky Perc Devlin looked hostilely at Smith. 'Didn't you understand,' he said. 'We aren't ordinary cowboys. Seems to me you take a heap of convincin'. Maybe you need to be caught flat-footed, disarmed, and marched another seven miles to get it through your bone-head, mister. We'll match Graeme with anything he wants to toss our way. We already have, or haven't you been listenin' to the talk around here about what happened to Lewis an' your bunk-mates last night?'

Smith studied Devlin silently for a moment before answering. 'Sure I listened,' he exclaimed. 'But you're havin' trouble separating luck from facts, pardner. You out-smarted King Lewis once. You out-smarted the rest o' us once too, at JG. But you'll never be that . . .'

'Oh hell,' growled Devlin exasperatedly, looking helplessly over at Buck. 'How do you talk sense to a numbskull?'

Smith's jaws snapped closed, his eyes blazed from their pouches of puckered flesh and his lips drew out cruelly thin. 'Feller,' he said softly, 'I'm goin' to remember you. We'll have another meetin' one o' these days—when I got a gun too.'

Devlin stiffened. He would have taken a step forward but Buck restrained him with two words. 'Hold it!' Devlin stopped but he did not turn away from the cold glare of Smith.

'Go get some rest,' Buck told Smith. 'I'm not saying you're not right, but what's happened so far wasn't just luck. I reckon you'll find that out one of these days, Smith. Now go on.'

As the towering gunfighter turned to shuffle away Percy Devlin said a fierce word. 'One of these times just walk away,' he said to Buck. 'That big lump of lard's got a little humbling comin'.'

Buck was studying the sun and made no comment about this. Afternoon was settled

118

upon the land now; the heat was unnerving; it was a solid force which pressed upon men and animals leeching away energy and initiative.

'Hey,' an identifiably garrulous voice called from under the cook-wagon texas. 'There's a sift of dust yonder to the south. Looks like maybe a rider or two comin' on from that pass up out o' here.'

Devlin yanked down his hatbrim to aid in peering ahead. Buck didn't bother to even look; he started over where his saddled horse stood asleep in wagon-shade. He snugged up the rigging, stepped up and reined around.

'You want me to come along?' Perc called.

Buck wagged his head and kept on riding. He too had seen that narrow pillar of dust; it could not be made by more than one rider, at the most, two riders. He had no intention of loping into trouble and with all that land around to manoeuvre in, he was confident he could not be caught, if that was anyone's intention.

But secretly, in a dark part of his mind, he did not believe that was trouble riding into his valley at all. He thought it was something else altogether so he kept on riding southward watching those little dry dust-devils ahead until he could make out that only one rider was approaching. He angled over near the river keeping to tree and willow shade there until, later, he could discern the look of that oncoming traveller.

119

He dismounted near a towering old cottonwood, watered his horse, tied it out of sight in a willow thicket, made a smoke and leaned there with his hat back, his bronzed face forward, waiting until the rider was close enough for identification. Then, when the rider would have passed on by, he called out, catching the person's quick attention.

' 'Afternoon, Miss Kate.'

Old Graeme's daughter looked over her shoulder at him, seeing him only after a little effort where he blended with willow-shadows. She reined towards him without acknowledging that greeting; hauled up less than twenty feet away and sat up there looking gravely into his face.

'My father says he underestimated you, Mister Handley.' Kate showed poise and a depth of solid calmness; she reminded him right then of her father. The same ironness of spirit was there confronting him. The identical minimal use of words. The same bold and assessing stare.

'That's a common mistake people make,' he said. 'Not just with me; with other people generally.'

'What did you do with my father's new hands?'

'Gunmen you mean, don't you?'

She said nothing, just sat there waiting for him to answer, her face heat-flushed and more beautiful in his eyes than usual, but otherwise showing no awareness of the murderous heat.

'Come into the shade,' he suggested.

She did this. She also dismounted and let him lead her animal down to the river for a drink. She did not watch him do this but he never once took his gaze off her. Not until he tied the horse near his own animal and afterwards walked back to her by the cottonwood tree.

'Your pappy's gunfighters are in my camp sleeping. They had a long walk from JG this morning.'

Kate's green gaze widened. 'You walked them on foot all the way here?'

Buck nodded. 'Easier than wakin' you up getting horses for them. Anyway, aside from one with sore feet and blisters, they made it all right.'

Kate continued to stare at him. 'What did you do with the others; with our rangeboss and our regular riders?'

He said, 'You knew, didn't you?'

'Knew what?'

'That they were going to hit our camp last night and stampede cattle over us.'

She did not deny this; she showed no surprise at what he said either, which was in itself, in Buck's view, an admission that she had known what JG had planned.

'Like father like daughter,' he murmured, and was displeased with her.

The bitterness of his steady look held her

121

interest exactly as his words, another time, had done this same thing. She said: 'What did you expect, Mister Handley; didn't you think we'd fight for what is ours by right of common usage?'

'Talk,' he said sharply to her. 'That's talk—a lot of words and nothing more. You know it, your father knows it, and I know it. Last night your JG outfit left off talking and went into action. Well, Miss Kate; I like that better myself. You folks want a war— I'm going to give you one.'

'All right,' she said back at him, then stopped, corrected herself and softened her tone to him. 'No. No, that's not what I meant to say. It's not what I rode over here to say.' She stopped again, looking straight at him. 'You have the ability to antagonise people. I suppose you know that, don't you, Mister Handley?'

'Only the people who're dead-set on walking over me, ma'm. I antagonise them because I don't take that kind of treatment lying down.'

She was not winning here and clearly she was accustomed to winning. Her lovely eyes narrowed, lost what little warmth they had just begun to show, and she said, 'We have more men, Mister Handley. We'll get even more if we have to.'

'You get them, Miss Graeme. You go ahead and get them. Did you know I can hire those men we captured at JG last night for the same pay your father offered them? Do you know what a fight like this evolves into? A range war, ma'm; the dirtiest kind of a fight men in the cattle business engage in. Not just shooting, but stampeding and burning and bushwhacking.'

She heard him out with perfect composure. His smoky gaze turned her away from him. She looked out where heatwaves shimmered, where blue-hazed distant ramparts stood under the merciless sun, and was totally unconscious how the half-light of this cool and benign place put its lush light over her, staining her cheeks, her throat, butter-yellow, and made her jet-black hair shine in a blue-black way.

'I rode over here,' she said, enunciating very distinctly as though speaking mechanically, as though she had rehearsed this on the ride from JG, which she had, 'to ask you once more to leave the Devil's Punch Bowl.' Then, before he could answer this, she whipped around and said in a more natural tone: 'But I can see that you won't do that, so now I'm asking you to stop this thing before it gets completely out of hand. Before it degenerates into exactly what you just said would happen:"

He looked at her. She had been cold to him. She had been angry with him. Now she was neither of these things. He could not help but notice the curve of her shoulders, the stark beauty of her features and that hot black brightness from her hair. The shape of her lips and the full, solid turnings of her body brought to life in him again that rich longing he'd felt in her presence before.

'I will do what I can,' he said. 'I've said before I don't want to fight JG. I even told you why—because the idea of you and I being on opposite sides struck me wrong. Dead wrong. But you've got to help. This can't be a one-way road, Miss Kate.'

She was candidly considering him now, considering him for his real character, his real worth. A little vagrant breeze came sighing down-river bringing with it a brief interlude of very pleasant coolness. She moved closer to the cottonwood tree where he stood; close enough to be touched and he wanted very much to touch her because the magic of her depthless calm, her extreme beauty and her solemnity struck through him, bringing all his long-felt hungers, all his lonely years apart from women of her kind, to a hard quickening, to a heady conclusion.

'Tell me of yourself,' she said quietly, not looking at him. 'Tell me what's made you as you are.'

'How am I?' he asked.

'Hard, uncompromising—courageous.' She turned. 'Not lucky; my father said you were a fool hung with luck. That's not right, Mister Handley. I know you better than my father

124

does. It's not luck.'

'What is it?'

She was looking into his face when she said, 'Boldness.' Her eyes were speculative and cool now; they were puzzled with him but drawn inexorably to him too.

He felt heat in his cheeks. 'How much boldness need a man have?' he murmured to her.

Her lips parted and remained that way. 'I don't know, really, Mister Handley. I've been waiting ten years to find out.'

'And you haven't, in all those years?'

She shook her head gently. 'Men come to JG and they go. I've never found the man yet.'

He put out both hands, let them rest upon her waist. He gently tilted her towards him, dropped his head and kissed her squarely on the mouth. For a second she was rigid, then she came to him burning him with her own kiss.

CHAPTER THIRTEEN

It was near evening when Kate Graeme left the Devil's Punch Bowl riding southward towards the pass. She would meet Buck again the next afternoon; meanwhile she would reason with her father. That was their agreement.

On his side, Buck had promised to do nothing until they met again. On the way back to camp he turned all that had happened between them there beside the river over and over in his mind. Experience told him not to trust her; not to trust anyone connected with JG. But something more potent inclined him to be patient, to stake his future on the grave promise of a beautiful, quiet-spoken green-eyed girl.

At the camp men were idly awaiting supper. Some looked inquiringly up as he rode in but none asked any questions, which was just as well because he'd have answered none. The men who had been out with the cattle were there; in fact for this little time before supper everyone was there including those fifteen captives from JG, most of whom had accepted their plight stoically and were acting no different than the pothook riders also acted, for that was the way with men; given enough time to discover mutual interests enemies often became, if not fast friends, then at least tolerant acquaintances.

The man called Smith, stepping gingerly around in stocking feet took a good deal of ribbing from both factions. He acknowledged none of this, yet it was plain to see that he didn't really mind. He was a man's man among his own kind and he was therefore at ease despite his status as a prisoner. When Burton Riddle bawled out that supper was ready

Smith went forward with a tin plate, a tin cup, and a loose grin.

'Eats like a horse,' Laramie Potter told Percy Devlin.

'Big as one too,' retorted Perc, watching Smith.

'Of the lot I think he's pretty regular.'

'Yeah; for a gunfighter.' Perc kept appraising Smith. 'He offered to fight me this afternoon. What d'you think of that?'

'Nothin',' answered Laramie. 'He did the same to me.'

'And?'

Laramie looked over where Smith was easing down cross-legged to eat. He said frankly: 'I'm just as glad it didn't come off. He's no easy mark from the looks of him.'

Buck came over to these two with his plate, his solemn expression, and eased down in wagon-shade. They could both see that something was on his mind so neither of them spoke for a long time, not until everyone was eating and there was a kind of absorbing silence over the camp. Then Devlin said: 'Buck; I expect some of us'll have to go huntin' in the mountains tomorrow if we're goin' to keep these prisoners. Riddle told me he didn't have enough supplies to feed 'em indefinitely.'

Buck nodded over this and kept on eating without speaking. Devlin and Potter exchanged a look.

Summertime evenings in the high country

lingered; there was none of that sudden-swift falling of night one met with down on the deserts. For hours, usually until after nine o'clock, daylight remained. This was the good time of day, for excepting dawn it was cool and clear and pleasant. After sunset the direct burning rays vanished, the earth sighed up its burden of daytime heat, and heat-smoke turned red with a soft-saffron coolness which did not change much until the small hours of the ensuing pre-dawn, when a little chill came to freshen things.

The pothook men completed their meal, hiked along to the river-bank in pairs, in threesomes, to cleanse their cups and plates, to smoke and idly converse, to wander over to the rope-corral to care for the saddle-stock, to take the measure of things and compare judgements. But whatever they did, they did not go far from their wagon-camp. No one was out with the cattle now, and later, after the nighthawks had ridden off, there would be the eternal monte and poker games by candlelight, but that wouldn't be for some time yet; not until darkness came.

Burton Riddle came over to Buck while the men were tossing their tinware into the tailgate-chuck-box, and said essentially what Perc Devlin had also said about a need existing for them to augment their provisions with buck meat or antelope or bear steaks and roasts.

'Just too blamed many mouths to feed,

Buckley. We didn't bargain for so many when we stocked up back in the settlements.'

'All right; tomorrow I'll send out hunting parties. It's nothing to worry about, Burt.'

'I'm not worrying,' Riddle exclaimed. 'Only takin' prudent precaution not to get caught short. Funny thing about rangemen—they'll take an awful lot from their cook, but let him run low on chuck an' overnight he ain't their friend an' father-confessor no more, he's their enemy. Sort o' like it is with a man an' wife when the woman don't cook good. The romance goes up in smoke.'

Buck raised his eyes to Riddle's face. 'How do you know how it is between a man and his wife; 'you been married, Burt?'

'Yes,' said the cook, his testy eyes filming over a little and his face losing some of its show of temper. 'Yes, I was married, Buck. For ten years.' Riddle sat down in the dirt. 'She died. Right near the end o' the war she got took with the grippe an' died.'

Buck stirred. 'I'm sorry,' he murmured. 'I didn't mean to poke around, Burt.'

'Now, boy, you weren't pokin' around. A man don't forget a good woman—ever. Maybe he never speaks of her but she's always there an inch or two under his other thoughts.' Riddle looked at the ground; he traced out the initials C.R. in dust, and he softly smiled over something private; the smile broadened and he suddenly looked up again, his eyes bright and

129

boyish-looking.

'I used to tease her. Y'see, her name was Cynthia an' she came from a powerful church-goin' family. I used to call her Cyn for short and she'd turn red as a rose and scowl at me.'

Riddle chuckled.

'Now that don't seem much, does it? Well; it's little kind of pointless things like that which make a marriage, Buckley. The big decisions, even the crises, seem to take care o' themselves—but it's the little things a feller never forgets.'

Riddle suddenly checked himself; he placed both hands upon the ground to arise and he said self-consciously, 'Hell; what'm I doin'—sittin' here like an old fool in his dotage talkin' about stuff that couldn't interest you at . . .'

'Wait,' Buck said quickly. 'Go on, Burt.'

'Go on?'

'Yeah.'

Those two looked long at one another. Riddle, looking for Handley's reason in this matter, thought he found it when he ultimately eased back down, saying: 'Yeah; a feller gets lonely; he has his dreams. Well; whether they ever come to anythin' or not maybe isn't too important—so long as he has 'em.' He nodded, liking the sound of this. 'Marriage is sort of like livin' in Texas: It's not *being* married so much as it's the state of mind. A feller belongs to someone when he's got a good woman; whatever he does he's thinkin' of her when he

130

does it.' Riddle's face pinched up into the expression frequently used by men who felt things which they had difficulty expressing.

When old Riddle paused Buck said: 'You could have married again, Burton.'

'Naw, boy. You've never been through it or you wouldn't say that. First off—it wouldn't be fair to the second wife because a man's sort of like the Canada honker; he mates for life. If his woman's good, no matter what comes next he can't ever forget how it was between 'em. Naw! for me anyway it'd never work. I know there are fellers it don't much bother—one wife or two—but not for me and not for you.'

Buck looked surprised. 'Not for me?' he echoed.

Riddle shook his head. 'We've been together quite a spell. I figure I know you pretty well. You an' Hoyt too, for that matter. Old Hoyt's just plain not the marryin' kind.'

'But I am?'

'Yes. It's always sort of secretly interested me—seein' just how long you'd go on bein' a free-grazer. You're not the nomad type really. It's in you like it used to be in me, to have a home, a woman, kids, a herd of cattle and a band of good horses—all on your own piece of land. You've been a drifter, sure; lots of us have been since the war, Buckley, but it ends some day for most of us—one way or another it ends.'

Buck was staring at Riddle. As old Burt had

said, they'd been together a long time, and yet this was the first time in all those years he had the feeling that he actually knew Burton Riddle.

'What you starin' at?' asked the camp-cook, beginning to stiffen into his usual attitude of testiness.

'You, Burt. You're quite a man.'

'Oh hell,' said the cook in quick embarrassment. 'My biggest trouble is that I talk too much.' He swiftly stood up, winced as his bad leg momentarily pained him, cleared his throat and said, 'Well; just don't forget to send those hunters out tomorrow.'

Buck sat there watching Riddle walk back to his wagon. Was still like that when Buff Evans came over and said, 'This is a pretty popular place; more riders comin' down from the pass, Buck.'

It took a moment for Handley to bring his thoughts back to the present; he did not acknowledge what Buff said for a few seconds, then he rose up off the ground, turned silently and looked southward. It was impossible to see anything now though, with those long shadows over the valley, and Evans, anticipating Buck's thoughts, said, 'Couple o' the boys come in from the herd to warn us.'

'Did they say who the riders were?'

'No; didn't get that close to 'em. Only said there was about ten of 'em.'

'All right, Buff. Have the prisoners rounded

132

up and herded northward up along the river under strong guard. If it's trouble we don't want them amongst us.'

'All right.'

'One more thing; pass the word—no trouble unless I say so. The boys can take positions around the wagons with Winchesters.'

'If it's no more'n ten men, Buck, it's probably old Graeme with more talk. He wouldn't dare start nothin' with no more gunhands than that, would he?'

'Wait and see,' said Buck. 'Now go on, get things ready. And, Buff—send Laramie and Perc Devlin out here to me with their carbines. Have Fred Naylor head for the men out with the cattle and fetch them back to camp.'

Evans moved quickly towards the wagons. Over there, several riders were already aware of an impending visit by unknown riders and a ripple of quiet excitement was beginning to run through the camp. The man calling himself Smith, noticing the altered attitude, tugged on his boots and started out where Buck was standing, facing the south. Buff Evans called after him.

'Hey, you—get back here.'

'Make me,' growled the big man, and kept on walking.

Buck heard him coming and turned. He looked unpleasantly at Smith but he did not speak until Smith had.

'Mister Handley; this idlin' around here is

sort of pree-judicial to m'health. If there's trouble comin' I'd rather have a hand in it, an' I figure you can use another hand; 'specially an experienced hand.'

Buck's initial reaction was to sharply decline this offer of aid as he'd previously done. He was, in fact, on the verge of doing this when Smith said something which brought Buck's attention up anew.

'JG's not just hirin' men, Mister Handley, it's hirin' the best. Like King Lewis's old pardner from Texas—The Uvalde Kid. Now, I know the Kid too, an' I been thinkin' that if . . .'

'Are you certain about that?' Buck asked sharply.

'About the Uvalde Kid? Sure I'm sure. Like I was just saying, I know the Kid pretty well myself. He told me about JG lookin' for men; that's how come me to ride there for a job.'

Smith said more but Buck was no longer listening. It struck him forcibly that Kate would probably have known this, yet she had said nothing about it to him. In the wake of this bitter reflection came another just as bitter: If she'd deliberately withheld this from him, she had not done it accidentally. No one overlooked mentioning as notorious a frontier gunfighter as the Uvalde Kid; he was known from Texas's panhandle to Montana's badlands.

Smith stopped speaking; he squinted his eyes and stared beyond Buck where a dark

134

sifting of mountain-shadow gloom lay. When next he spoke Buck heard him; heard the quickly altered tone he was using now as much as the words themselves.

'Speak of the devil . . . Damned if it's not the Kid himself.'

Buff Evans came striding up, Winchester carbine hooked over one arm. Behind him came Laramie Potter and Percy Devlin, similarly armed.

Buff said: 'Smith; get back to the wagons. I'll not tell you again!'

Buck had turned away at Smith's words to gaze upon the little party of approaching horsemen. He recognised Jethro Graeme and King Lewis at once. He also saw familiar faces among the other JG men, but the one rider he singled out for his personal attention was a sun-darkened very thin man, tall, taller even than Devlin or Laramie Potter. This man was the notorious Uvalde Kid; his face had at one time or another decorated law enforcement posters from one end of the west to the other end.

When Evans snarled again at the man called Smith, bringing Buck around, there was no time for further talk. The JG men were within gunshot-distance and were slowing as they saw the free-grazers standing there ahead of them in the dusk.

'Never mind,' said Buck to Evans. 'Let Smith stay for now. And, boys—watch yourselves; that man on old Graeme's left is the Uvalde Kid.'

Potter, Evans and Devlin started where they stood, forgetting Smith to throw quick looks outward where Graeme was halting with his riders up around him, with the Uvalde Kid up abreast of him looking blankly down.

'Handley,' old Jethro said, 'I made a promise today. I'm here this evening to fulfil it.' He paused to look steadily at Buck. His tough features were set in an unrelenting way, but still, in Buck's view, there was a lot about this hard old man that was reminiscent of his daughter.

'I promised Kate I'd have a final talk with you. That's all I promised her.'

Buck and the men with him were like stone. King Lewis, his face twisted with rage and hatred, looked away from Buck only one time; that was when he sighted the gunman called Smith standing back by Laramie Potter and Buff Evans. Lewis saw Smith's empty holster; he also saw the bleak look on Smith's face and this seemed to perplex him briefly. Then he switched that look of savage hatred back on Buck again, ignoring Smith and the others who were standing there.

Graeme leaned a little in his saddle. 'I keep my word, Handley. I'm here and I'm going to talk—but nothing's changed between us. You leave the Punch Bowl afoot, astride, or dead and laid out—it's all the same to me, but you

136

leave.'

Buck looked from Graeme to the gaunt, sun-darkened tall man beside him. ' 'You buying in too?' he asked the Uvalde Kid.

For a little time no answer came back to this. The notorious gunfighter's gaze lifted beyond Buck, settled upon the man called Smith, and lingered there. 'Which side you on in this?' he quietly asked.

Smith lifted his shoulders and let them fall. 'You know me,' he said back. 'I'm on the side I like best.'

'Yeah,' grunted the Uvalde Kid. 'You always were a hard one to figure. Well—which side, Bull?'

'Why; what difference does it make, Kid?'

Uvalde reached up, scratched his jaw, and said laconically, 'We can't be on opposite sides, Bull. You know that.'

Jethro Graeme swung his head. So did King Lewis and the other JG riders. Jethro said bleakly: 'You're taking my pay, Kid. You remember that.'

Uvalde did a surprising thing. He fished into a shirt-pocket, brought forth a little wad of paper currency, looked old Graeme straight in the eye and threw the money down upon the ground. He didn't say a word, but after a moment longer of exchanging looks with Jethro he gazed ahead at Smith again.

'You're always doin' stupid things,' he said, drew in a long breath, let it out and lifted his

137

rein hand. 'All right; I know which side you're takin' and as usual I think you're crazy, but I guess it'll have to be that way.'

No one said a word. The Uvalde Kid kneed his horse away from beside Jethro Graeme, rode on over where Smith was standing, reversed the animal and sat there looking without any expression at all over at Graeme, King Lewis, and the JG men. Graeme's face paled with anger but it was King who spoke.

'Uvalde; what the hell are you doing?'

'Changin' sides. Graeme's money is there on the ground.'

'But hell,' Lewis protested loudly. 'You can't do that; we already talked about this free-graze scum. You agreed to . . .'

'I changed my mind, King.'

Lewis sat there with his mouth open; he seemed stunned at this totally unexpected turn of events. Jethro Graeme did not react in the same way. He kept staring at Uvalde. Finally he said: 'Answer me one question: Why; do any of these free-grazers have any hold on you?'

'Not particularly,' drawled the Kid. 'But this feller here without any gun . . .'

'He works for me,' broke in Jethro. 'Handley here abducted him last night along with fourteen other men I hired.'

The Uvalde Kid nodded. 'So I heard tell,' he retorted. 'But you see, I know this feller pretty well. I know which side he's on even if he's reluctant to say, and because of that I can't rightly take your money.'

'Why not?' demanded King Lewis hotly. 'What's wrong with you, Uvalde; that man's a prisoner here. Anyway, what's he to you?'

Buck was also wondering this same thing where he stood momentarily forgotten by Jethro Graeme and dark King Lewis, gazing with surprise up at the tall, thin gunfighter.

'It's a long story,' said the Kid to King Lewis. 'It goes back a long way. Bull and I grew up together. After a few years our trails parted.' Uvalde raised his shoulders and let them fall. 'We didn't see things the same way, King. Now you and I—we did see things the same way—right up until the day you sold Billy Thompson to those Kansans for gold. After that, I sort of cut you off my list too.'

'What,' Buck interrupted to ask, 'does any of this have to do with Smith here?'

'Smith? Oh; you mean Bull here. Well now, feller, it's like this: Bull is my *brother.*'

Every man there was dumbfounded. Buck, looking at Smith, saw the large, scarred gunfighter cast a sidelong glance at the Uvalde Kid, then look away again.

Someone breathed softly: 'I'll be damned.'

CHAPTER FOURTEEN

Jethro Graeme recovered first. He continued to stare at the Uvalde Kid for a long time before dropping his gaze briefly to Smith, then bringing it even closer, to Buck Handley.

'Like I told Kate,' he growled. 'You're hung with horseshoes, Handley. You're just plain lucky.' He lifted his reins. 'All right; by a fluke you've won this meeting too. I brought that turn-coat over here to kill you. Now it's got to be done a different way. But as I told you—I keep my word. I'll see you dead if it's the last thing I ever do and that's final.'

Graeme jerked his animal around, snarled an order at the men with him, booted his animal into a lope and went rocketing back the way he had come. The last of his men to depart was King Lewis; he continued to stare unbelievingly at the Uvalde Kid after the others had gone, then he too ultimately departed.

The man called Smith said to the Uvalde Kid: 'How come you not to tell that old firebrand who I was? He surely told you I was at JG—that I was one of the men captured by these free-grazers.'

Uvalde dismounted, relinquished his reins to Percy Devlin, and said, 'Bull—how the hell was I to know the man old Graeme called

Smith was you? When he reined up out there you could have knocked me off that damned horse with a feather. There you were big as life, twice as ugly, and without your gun—but showin' in every line of you that you were favourin' these free-grazers.'

'You told me about JG needin' men the last time we met a few days back down in . . .'

'Sure I told you, you overgrown numbskull. And I expected to find you at JG too. But then what did I find; you over here lookin' daggers at King and that crusty old cowman.'

Buck walked over, considered the Uvalde Kid briefly and said, 'Was that true; did Graeme bring you over here to kill me?'

Uvalde turned a little to look at Buck. 'He didn't say anything about that at all until you heard him. Not to me at any rate. But if he had it wouldn't have changed anything; I wouldn't have tried it in front of all the men you've got slippin' around here with Winchesters.'

Over at the wagons Buff, Percy and Laramie were telling the other pothook riders who that tall, thin man was. Every head was turned towards the place where Smith, Buck, and the notorious Texan stood. Burton Riddle, the only one to speak into the hush around his wagon, said, 'Yeah,' pithily, 'I've seen him before. 'Saw him kill a greaser gunfighter down in Laredo one time. I'll tell you, boys, if he's got to be in this fight I sure give thanks it's *fer* us an' not ag'in us.'

Laramie turned, saying softly: 'Poke up the fire, Burton, they'll likely want coffee.' Then he bent a look over at Perc Devlin to say in a different voice: 'How do you like that; Smith is his brother. Beats all, don't it?'

Devlin allowed that it did indeed 'beat all', then he stepped ahead to help Riddle with the fire as Buck, the Uvalde Kid, and the man called Smith strode up and halted. Smith looked glum but the Kid seemed perfectly at ease. He ran a hawk-like glance once around at those discreetly retreating cowboys, nodded and eased down where Buck also sat.

Buck called out: 'Percy; go fetch the prisoners back. There'll be no trouble tonight.'

When Burt Riddle brought three cups of black coffee Smith looked up at him, muttered 'Thanks' and looked down again. Buck noticed this.

'What's wrong with you?' he asked.

Before Smith could answer the Kid said wryly: 'Oh; he's always like that when I'm around. You see; the only man who ever consistently beat my brother to the draw is me. Every time we meet we unload and try each other. In the past ten years we've run across one another at least fifty times and it always ends the same way. I beat him.'

'With guns,' growled Smith, looking balefully at the Uvalde Kid. 'I could tie you in knots with my hands.'

Uvalde smiled. 'But I don't fight with fists,
142

Bull, and you'll never be man enough to whip me with guns, so drink your coffee and rest easy.'

'I can't pay you what Graeme offered,' said Buck. 'I can't even hire you, Uvalde, because I've got a policy—no professional gunfighters.'

Uvalde looked over at his brother with raised eyebrows. 'If that's the case, just what the hell did you pick this side for?' he demanded.

'It just so happens,' retorted Smith fiercely, 'that I pick the side I like an' the pay's never had a whole lot to do with it, and you blamed well know that, too.'

Uvalde drank, shrugged, lowered his cup and said to Buck, 'Turn 'em loose, Handley. You can't hold all fifteen of 'em.'

Buck shook his head. 'Not as long as Jethro Graeme'll hire them right back again.'

'He won't re-hire 'em.'

'How do you know that?'

'Easy,' said Uvalde. 'I'll have a little talk with each of them. I'll promise you none of 'em will go back to JG.'

Uvalde's voice had a silky overtone to it which made his unspoken promise even more lethal than his spoken one. His brother, evidently recognising this tone, made a dour face.

'The fast gun,' he snidely said. 'Mister Handley; you're sittin' next to the little tin god of Texas.'

143

Uvalde ignored this. He was peering ahead where those JG men were walking back into camp. He snorted and said, 'Hell, Bull; is that what you run with nowadays—men like that?'

'You hired out to JG too.'

Uvalde, having scored, wagged his head. 'Not if I'd seen what old Graeme was hirin' I wouldn't have.'

'Yeah; how about your old pardner, Lewis?'

Uvalde looked into his coffee cup. He seemed to be considering his answer. Finally he said, 'King's like all the rest of us. He was a pretty good man until the sweet stink of two thousand dollars made him what he is now.' Uvalde put aside the cup and looked at Buck. 'Never mind King Lewis right now. How about it, Handley; you going to turn 'em loose?'

Buck narrowed his eyes wondering whether or not to trust this notorious gunfighter. It was Smith who resolved the enigma for him. Smith said, 'His word's good, Buck. Not much else about him is, but at least his word's good. If he says they won't re-hire out to old Graeme, they won't.'

'Thanks,' said Uvalde, eyeing his brother sardonically. 'Tell me, Handley, did you ever see brothers so fond of each other before?'

Buck felt like laughing over this, and he did. Uvalde grinned a little; even Smith chuckled. Smith said, 'When the others go, you ride out too.'

Uvalde didn't hesitate a moment; he

144

nodded total agreement. 'The pay's no good, the coffee's too weak, I never liked wagon-camps, and if Mister Handley doesn't want gunfighters around that's fine with me.'

Uvalde stood up, he was a head taller than either his brother or Buck. 'You goin' to turn 'em loose?' he asked again.

Buck said, 'Yes; on your terms. They won't run right back to JG.'

'Well; they'll have to go back after their gatherings and their horses, but I'll ride along with 'em. They won't stay at JG, I promise you that.'

Buck sobered. 'What about you; the minute you show up back at JG Lewis and Graeme'll sick their other gunhands on you.'

'Naw,' said Uvalde scornfully. 'You'd be surprised what a good reputation will save you from.'

'Good!' exploded Smith. 'Good; why hell's bells, of all the blasted danged conceit I ever ...'

'Bull,' broke in Uvalde, 'your jealousy is showin', boy.' He smiled, looked around for his horse, saw where Devlin had tethered the beast, nodded once to Buck and walked away. Where Smith stood darkly watching Uvalde stride onward, he said a coarse word.

Buck, considering these two, shook his head. 'How is it that you dislike him so and he seems to also dislike you—yet when there was a good chance you two could take opposite sides in a range war, he wouldn't be on the

145

other side?'

'That's simple,' growled Smith, still watching his brother where the Uvalde Kid was mounting up and reining towards those fifteen herded-together captives. 'We're brothers. Brothers can't actually shoot at one another.'

'Only with their mouths, is that it?'

Smith swung to face Buck. He very gradually let a little grin settle around his lips. 'Naw; not really,' he said. 'Sure I get mad at him. He's too overbearin' for my taste. But it's just talk—all that stuff between us.'

'Tell me one thing about him, Smith. Is he what folks say he is?'

Smith sobered at once. He swung his head to consider the Uvalde Kid where he was sitting his saddle talking to the JG men. In a very quiet tone of voice Smith said: 'Yes, he's a killer. I reckon, if we've really got any major difference, that's it.'

'But you hire your gun out too.'

'Not for money, Mister Handley. Not the way *he* does. If I was like that I wouldn't be standin' here with you now, I'd be over with the other JG lads. We've argued about that. Really argued.' Smith stopped speaking. He kept watching his brother. He obviously was going to say no more, nor did he.

Buck stood there near Smith watching Uvalde herd those sullen captives out into the southward evening; was still watching some little time later when the Uvalde Kid twisted, threw back a casual wave, then faded out with his walking companions. Buck did not return that wave. Neither did the man who called himself Smith.

Fred Naylor came up, along with Perc Devlin, Buff Evans and several other pothook riders. Instead of saying what clearly was in all their curious minds though, after one look at the expressions of Smith's and Buck's faces Naylor said only: 'You want to put the nighthawks back out now, or not?'

Buck nodded his head at Fred. He then reached forth to brush a hand over Smith's arm to attract the larger man's attention, and he said quietly, 'We pay thirty a month and found, if you want to hire on as a cowboy—not as a gunfighter.'

'What gun,' growled Smith, at long last turning away from his southerly vigil. 'I don't even have a gun.' Smith looked steadily at Buck, 'All right; it's fair pay for a rider.' He afterwards stalked away from all of them.

'Leave him alone,' said Buck to the others. 'Give him until morning to come around.'

From far out a man's voice lifted in song came to the wagon-camp. Naylor said, 'I sent some boys out a while back, but only two of 'em. I'll send more out with 'em.' He walked away. Gradually all of them drifted along, some to the poker game going on at Riddle's wagon, others to their blankets, and a few just to walk out a way into the soft pure night and be alone for a while.

Buck did that; he went over to the river and sat there upon a bleached deadfall-cottonwood, his mind alive to the kaleidoscope of events which had touched his life one way or another this day, robbing him of any wish for rest despite his tiredness.

The San Juan showed silvery crests upon its little rolling waves where starshine came upon it. It made its ancient soothing sound and raised up its dank coolness in the night.

Buck made a smoke, lit it and blew out.

He'd wronged Kate; she hadn't known about the Uvalde Kid. She couldn't have known or she wouldn't have been satisfied to only plead with her father. It made him feel so much better finding it possible to affirm to himself his faith in her once more. She had, only this day, come to mean so very much to him.

He inhaled, exhaled.

Old Burt Riddle was right; in every man's heart there is an image, a dream of what he wants from life. Buck had it; it was the dream Burt Riddle had said it was.

CHAPTER FIFTEEN

The following day was quiet in the Devil's Punch Bowl. Buck sent out two sentries to the hillock on across the river; he sent the daytime riders out to the herd. Morning came and went with nothing happening of much consequence; the heat was blast-furnace-like as usual from ten o'clock on. He sat in for a while with Smith and the nighthawks at a monte layout, then, when the heat bore down the nighthawks sought their bedrolls beneath wagons and dozed off. Smith went to the river, bathed his feet, returned to camp, got a horse and rode out to the herd.

Burton Riddle was making a pot-pie with sweat darkening his shirt, front and back. Just before high noon two men rode in who had left before dawn to hunt in the easterly hills. They had an antlered buckdeer with them and a pronghorn antelope. Riddle's lined face creased into the first genuine smile of the day at sight of these welcome additions to his dwindling larder. Buck's last view of those three was down by the river where they'd pulled both carcasses up by lariat to low-hanging tree limbs and were systematically skinning and gutting each animal. He rode out of camp southward-bound with the sun a little off-centre, hearing in a diminishing way the casual talk of those three men at their work.

The valley's grass was beginning to flake-out now, to cure on the stem as all wild grasses do, being at best and regardless of rainfall in that hot, high country, only a sixty-day crop. But there was more than enough graze here to supply the cattle on into a late Fall, and after that failed there was the browse; the buck-brush, rip-gut, cottonwood leaves and limbs which sustained animals far into the winter, each year, sometimes carrying them through into the following spring.

As he rode along considering these things, the way every lifelong cowman does, he could not avoid the feeling secret valleys like this one were rapidly being discovered and settled. They were the kind of treasure every cowman sought; places where high mountains ringed round a deep-soil valley protecting the flat lands from winter's worst freezes and drifting snows. To men who put up no hay, had neither the equipment nor the inclination to do so, a place like the Devil's Punch Bowl was priceless.

'Worth fighting for,' he told his horse, speaking aloud as most lonely men do. 'Worth settling in.'

It was past one o'clock when he came to the buck-run in the eastern foothills leading up to that wider mule-trail where he'd first encountered Kate Graeme. It never occurred to him as he set his mount to climbing that she might not be there.

Here, upon the front wall of a dark mountain the heat was bearable; it was reflected outward and downward. After he came to the pack-trail, which was wide enough for two riders abreast, there were even occasional dark shadows to pass through. Below lay the full run of the valley flowing onward under its heat-haze for miles southward and westward. The San Juan, chocolate-coloured and sluggish, swirled southward in its thick and oily way. Along its banks where trees and willows grew there lay a soft, filigreed shade-pattern which constantly changed. Taken in total the view from Buck's vantage point was sufficient to re-affirm what he'd told his horse: To own such an empire as the Devil's Punch Bowl a man would be willing to fight, and fight hard.

He came to that thrusting promontory where the trail made its long-spending curve, passed around it and immediately caught movement on ahead from the edge of his eye; a horse was drowsily standing there swishing its tail.

He saw Kate seated upon that smooth boulder again, and although he knew she'd heard him coming she did not at once look up; not until he reined up, stepped down, walked towards her and said, 'Your father said he keeps his word; I see you also keep yours.'

She stood up twisting to face him. There

was a sad look to her face, a strange deepening of the greeny colour to her eyes.

'He told me what happened last evening at your camp between the Uvalde Kid and the man called Smith.'

Buck pushed back his hat, moved into shade and said, 'Did you see Uvalde return to the ranch with the men we took from JG?'

'Uvalde didn't ride in with them.' At Buck's quick look of inquiry, Kate said, 'No; he told them what to do, then he waited out on the plain for them. He told them he would be watching when they rode off, and if all fourteen didn't leave JG he'd make it a point to hunt them down.'

Buck made a wry smile. 'And, did all fourteen quit?'

Kate matched his humourless smile with one just as ironic. 'Yes; they all quit. King was furious, but my father paid them off without a word. He was as mad as I've ever seen him but he didn't open his mouth to any of them.'

Buck said nothing; he kept his gaze fixed upon the beautiful girl. She, in turn, did not look away from him nor lower her eyes, and when she spoke again it was clear from her tone that her thoughts were not upon her words.

'How did you bring that off?'

'Luck. That time it was purest luck. I had no idea who Smith was. Of course I'd heard of the Uvalde Kid, but I didn't even know he had a

152

brother. Maybe your father was right—maybe I am just lucky.'

'You're going to have to be, Buck. My father doesn't accept defeat. It only makes him more determined.'

'Sure,' said Buck easily, 'I understand that. I admire him for it. If he hadn't had that kind of grit he wouldn't be as big and powerful as he is. But I'm kind of determined too; that's why I'm still here.'

'Is that the only reason, Buck?'

He looked at her and softly wagged his head. 'Maybe originally it was, but not now. Not since that first time I saw you up here. But especially not since yesterday, Kate.' He cocked his head a little at her. 'Tell me; you once told me that the men in this country come and go; that you'd never found the particular man for you. Do you think that's still true?'

She smiled at him, a genuinely wholesome smile. 'I don't think it's still true, no.' She looked down then up again. 'I'll be very frank with you; I didn't think that after we first met up here.'

'You sure didn't show it that first time.'

Her smile lingered. 'You don't understand women very well, Buck. Of course I didn't let you know that first time. What would you have thought of me if I had?'

'The same thing I think of you right now.'

'No,' she said, stepping over into shade was

153

beside him. 'No you wouldn't have.'

'Kate, I . . .'

'Buck, I've got to tell you something. Two things in fact. One of them is that our rangeboss has sworn he's going to kill you any way that he can. You made a fool of him; first by whipping him in front of my father and our riders, and again when you out-smarted him the night he led that attack upon your camp.'

Buck brought forth his tobacco sack and went to work silently manufacturing a smoke. He did not speak.

'The other thing I must tell you is that I can't be on both sides.'

He lit up, exhaled and swung to look at her. 'I wouldn't want that,' he murmured. 'All I want is for you to stay out of this. Just stand back and wait until it's over.'

'Until you're dead, Buck?'

He considered the tip of his cigarette through narrowed eyes. 'What I want, Kate,' he said very slowly, 'is worth taking that risk for.' He considered telling her where Hoyt McElroy had gone, but in the end, because of what she'd said about her loyalties, he did not tell her.

'What do you want—besides a season's free grass?'

'You, to begin with. And after that . . .'

'Yes; and after that?'

'Whatever you want to make out of life with me, Kate.'

She didn't colour; she didn't turn away from him. Her thoughtful gaze was suddenly very gentle and dark with strong yearning, but she kept looking at him. 'All this since yesterday, Buck?' she asked softly. 'After one kiss?'

'No; it's been coming a lot longer than that. But it's been the same with me it's been with you. I've been restless; I've been drifting first here then there. I've been searching for something.' He threw down the cigarette and stepped on it. 'It's been like a puzzle with me, Kate. I had most of the pieces in place, but two very important ones were missing. Then I rode into the Punch Bowl and found one of them. I rode up this trail and found the other one. It all fit together.' He lifted his face to her. 'Now, all I have to do is get possession and keep it.'

She wasn't smiling when she said, 'That's all? Just bring my father around—and me too?'

'Your father's hard, Kate. I don't particularly like him but I sure-Lord respect him. He's my kind of a man.'

She looked away, finally; put a sombre glance out over the drowsy land below. 'I said almost that same thing to him about you, Buck. I said the reason you two would fight was because you were the same kind of men. I made him promise to ride to your camp; to look at you as something more than an enemy: To talk to you.'

'He told me he'd promised you he'd ride

155

over.'

She swung abruptly towards him; they were less than a foot apart now. She said with sudden intentness: 'He didn't tell you the rest of it, though. I know he didn't because when he returned I went in and asked him.'

'The rest of what, Kate?'

Her breathing was uneven now, making her breasts rise and fall, making her eyes darker green than he'd ever before seen them. 'I'll answer your question in a moment,' she said, 'but first I want you to answer one for me: You said you wanted to make something from life with me.'

'Yes.'

'Put it plainer, Buck. Please.'

'I want to marry you, Kate. I can't make it any plainer. I'm in love with you.'

'Buck . . . would you leave the Punch Bowl for me?'

He hung there slowly breathing in, slowly breathing out. Her eyes locked with his; strange things lay in their deepest depths; he tried to define their meaning and failed. He looked beyond her finally, saying, 'I didn't think you'd do this to me, Kate. I don't know what to tell you.'

'Is it so difficult?'

'More than you know. For me, one thing goes with the other.'

'It's your pride, Buck. Your yeasty pride just as it is with my father.'

'No; there's some pride involved, but that's not it. It's disillusionment more than anything else. It never occurred to me you'd do this.'

She touched him. 'No woman who loves a man wants to see him torn apart like this. You don't have to answer.'

He moved from under her touch. 'I'll answer,' he muttered. 'I'll leave the valley, Kate. But *not* for you; I'll leave it to help me forget you.' He started around her towards his horse. His face was white.

For a stunned moment she looked after him. She had not thought it would go like this; that he would think of her what he now obviously did think. She moved; she ripped out his name and ran to where he was reaching for the reins to his horse. He was turning at the sound of her when she came close, put out both hands and expedited his facing around.

'I didn't ask you that question for the reason you think, Buck. Not at all. I asked it only to make certain in my own mind how much you really did care for me.'

He frowned down at her groping for understanding. Slowly he murmured: 'To see how much I cared? But Kate—I told you. I said I loved you, that I wanted to marry you.'

She shook her head desperately at him; she tightened her hold of his arms. 'Oh . . . but it's my fault. Please forgive me, Buck. I wanted to know which came first—the Punch Bowl or me. That's all I wanted to know.' She let him

157

go. 'I didn't really want you to leave. Do you see?'

He dropped the reins and reached roughly for her. She came close willingly; there was none of that brief coldness this time. She pressed into him full length and sought his mouth with her lips. She seared him with her passion and her want, then she pushed her face against him content to stay like that, and murmured:

'I'm shaking. Why is this so frightening?'

He had no ready-made answer, nor could he find one, so instead of replying he simply held her, conscious of the drum-roll of her heart, conscious of her closeness and her desirability, conscious too of the fragrance of her hair and also of the strange emotion which filled him to the exclusion of everything else. When some pebbles rattled down on to the trail from an overhead height he heard their little noise but did not bother to ascertain their reason for falling. The only thing in his mind at this moment was the girl in his arms.

Then the gunshot came.

Buck could not at once react to that totally unexpected explosion. A second passed, another second. Kate stiffened abruptly in his arms, then very gradually turned loose against him. A slight sound came from her throat. He tightened his grip as she began to wilt. The realisation that she had been shot stunned him. Two more seconds passed, then his muscles came alive; he caught her up with both arms, sprang back under the lee of the mountainside and flattened there. But there was only that one shot.

He put her gently upon the ground in a thin ribbon of mountainside shade. Her head rolled against his arm. She seemed lifeless to him. A spreading warmth spread slowly over his sleeve, saturating it. With gentle fingers he righted her head, probed beneath the wealth of jet hair and found where that blood was coming from. There was a long furrow half way up the left side of her head where a bullet had ploughed.

He ignored the thought of the unseen assassin's presence long enough to determine that Kate's wound was unlikely to prove fatal, then he made her as comfortable as possible, bandaged her head to staunch the flow of blood, and afterwards looked out where his horse stood. Across that exposed intervening distance the booted butt-plate of his carbine glinted; he wanted to make the run for that weapon but common sense warned him against this. Somewhere, overhead among the rimrocks, the unknown bushwhacker was undoubtedly waiting for him to make just such a move. Sweat ran into his eyes. He dashed it away, looked at Kate, saw her eyelids quiver and put a hand lightly upon her cheek. He did not believe she would regain consciousness so quickly despite her obvious unconscious will to do so. He did not want to leave her, and yet, because he thought he could do no more for her right then, he was eager to hunt down the man who had, he now reasoned, aimed at him and had hit her by mistake.

CHAPTER SIXTEEN

The day was no longer just hot; it now became evil in his sight. Fiercely hot and malevolent. He inched forward, drew his hand-gun and risked a look upwards.

There was nothing to be seen but those ancient dark and blisteringly-hot rimrocks; no sign of a man or of a gun-barrel. He waited a long time straining for a sight or a sound. He began to think the assassin had departed. But he never entirely accepted this; that bullet had been meant for him, the man who shot it would not give up now.

He threw rocks out into the trail to draw gunfire. None came. He placed his hat upon his pistol barrel and poked it far out where anyone overhead could see it. Still no shot came.

He sucked back, crushed the hat back on to his head and began a searching study of the mountainside south of him. That promontory around which the trail curved hid him from sight to the south. He ascended it step by step with his eyes, saw how a man could get to those overhead rocks, then balanced his chances. While he was climbing up there using both hands he would be at the mercy of anyone who saw him doing this, and who wished to kill him. But once he made it to the top-out there were random boulders of immense size which would amply protect him.

There was no other way. Going around by the trail would take hours. He had the time but he did not think Kate had it; whatever he decided, whatever he did, must be concluded within the next hour; Kate needed medical attention, but she also needed someone with her. He thought her unconsciousness might last an hour. Until that much time had passed he could do nothing for her anyway.

He made his decision, crept along the cliff-face as far as he dared, then holstered his six-gun and reached forth to begin climbing.

The stone face was hot to the touch. Sun-blast burnt into him making sweat run in streams under his clothing and downward from beneath his hat. Apprehension was solidly in him too; if he were seen spread-eagled upon the mountainside he could neither get away nor protect himself.

The first hundred feet were difficult. After that there were little crevices where swirling winter winds had deposited silt, and at these places tough manzanita, sage and chaparral grew. He used every sturdy plant which came was a sad look to her face, a strange deepening of the greeny colour to her eyes.

'He told me what happened last evening at your camp between the Uvalde Kid and the man called Smith.'

Buck pushed back his hat, moved into shade and said, 'Did you see Uvalde return to the ranch with the men we took from JG?'

'Uvalde didn't ride in with them.' At Buck's quick look of inquiry, Kate said, 'No; he told them what to do, then he waited out on the plain for them. He told them he would be watching when they rode off, and if all fourteen didn't leave JG he'd make it a point to hunt them down.'

Buck made a wry smile. 'And, did all fourteen quit?'

Kate matched his humourless smile with one just as ironic. 'Yes; they all quit. King was furious, but my father paid them off without a word. He was as mad as I've ever seen him but he didn't open his mouth to any of them.'

Buck said nothing; he kept his gaze fixed upon the beautiful girl. She, in turn, did not look away from him nor lower her eyes, and when she spoke again it was clear from her tone that her thoughts were not upon her words.

'How did you bring that off?'

'Luck. That time it was purest luck. I had no idea who Smith was. Of course I'd heard of the Uvalde Kid, but I didn't even know he had a

162

to hand as additional support.

Around him there was total silence. Once, a long way off, he heard a horse whistle; this sound seemed to come from directly under the mountainside but northward, about where that first buck-run led upwards from the valley floor.

Sweat stung his eyes. He flung it away annoyedly and continued to climb. He grabbed for a ragged plant, caught hold and groaned. The plant was a spiny cat-claw. When he was able, a little farther along, he teetered in space and drew forth the thorns from his hand. Blood came at once but instead of hindering him this moisture aided him in holding.

He had less than two hundred feet to go when that promontory dwindled up near the top-out leaving an exposed place to be crossed in full view from below as well as from above and northward; the direction of that gunshot which had so stunned him several minutes before. There was no other way to reach the rimrocks. He looked northward for his unknown foeman, for a flash of sunlight off metal, for anything which would tell him where the killer lay. He saw nothing at all but the eternal dark stone. He also looked downward; Kate lay exactly where he'd left her. She resembled a small broken doll from this height and the yonder valley was scarcely discernible at all through heat-haze and his sweat-blurred vision. He drew in a rattling big breath, caught two fresh hand-holds, and started the final upwards climb.

His heart thudded from exertion, thin and insufficient air made his lungs labour but desperation drove him fully sixty feet out into the open, steadily climbing towards those shielding rimrocks. Half way to the top he paused to catch his breath and dart quick looks round about, but it was only a momentary pause. Because of this, though, he survived what next occurred. He made two lunges upwards, each time pulling himself swiftly higher, and was therefore twice his own length onward when a gun exploded northerly, a lead slug flattened against stone where Buck had been moments before, throwing razor-sharp stone splinters in all directions.

There was no second shot. Buck threw his last reserves of strength into covering the final upward distance; he was certain of the reason why no second shot was fired. Whoever was up there with that carbine had belatedly discovered what Handley was doing; instead of risking another miss, that assassin was now springing up, running along the rim to the spot where Buck would top out, so that he could kill him at close range and before Buck could safely free one of his hands to fire back.

It was a race for survival; Buck knew that and strained every muscle to get in among the rimrocks before his enemy got above him first.

A man's hoarse outcry sounded. There was

a rattle among the rocks as though that unseen killer had fallen, had dropped his gun. Buck threw everything he had into crossing that perilous remaining distance. He was within twenty feet of the rim, was running a stabbing stare ahead where he would emerge seeking the killer, when another gunshot sounded. This one was much closer; the bullet however missed him and sang waspishly outward over the valley.

His enemy, instead of trying to complete his rush after tripping amid the rocks, was now prone with his carbine. He fired twice more. Each time his aim improved. Buck, realising that he would be struck soon, raised up, cramped both knees and sprang the last ten feet. He fell into a nest of bruising stones a fraction of a second ahead of another bullet. The sound of that slug passing was so clear he knew it could not have missed him by more than inches. Then he drew in his legs, dropped his head, and gulped in great amounts of air with a light-headed sensation holding him helpless for several minutes. Beyond his hiding place the rifleman ceased firing. Warnings flashed in Buck's mind; the killer would be stalking him; he had to hang on a little longer.

Now the silence descended again. At this considerable height no sound from the valley below could reach him, but the least sound made around him carried a surprising distance. That was how he knew he was being

165

stalked. It was the sound of leather dragging over stone, a whisper-soft abrasive sound, that urged him to fight against apathy; against the drowsy stupor all that fierce exertion under a pitiless sun had induced.

He drew his gun, finally, inched northward until he thought himself safe, and waited. That unseen stalker would have to expose himself, rising up over the rocks, to look down into the sunken place where Buck had topped-out. He waited and deeply breathed, and kept his cocked six-gun lightly resting across a steadying stone.

Time ran on. It was all in Buck's favour; he was able to completely recover, to lie easy until even his heart ceased its fierce beating and his gun-arm steadied.

That great depth of eerie silence was abruptly broken by a man's harsh outcry. The voice confirmed something which had occurred to Buck shortly after Kate's shooting. The man with the Winchester was King Lewis, old Jethro Graeme's rangeboss.

'All right, Handley,' called Lewis, and called Buck a fighting name. 'Stand up and fight, damn you. Stand up and fight!'

Buck remained totally still and quiet. He had placed the location of that voice; he corrected the aim of his six-gun and went on waiting.

'What's the matter, Handley; you scairt now? I thought you would be. I wish your riders could see you—cowering down in those rocks. I wish Uvalde could see you too.'

Buck drew in a breath. 'Lewis; you shot Kate. You missed me with that first bullet and hit Kate in the head.'

There was no reply to this for a long rime. Buck thought Lewis was placing him by his voice as he'd also done. He changed position crawling carefully northward. Then Lewis sang out again.

'That's tough, Handley. That's real tough. She's sweet on you, isn't she? I saw that; I knew it even before she told her old man.'

Buck twisted to drop flat. He wanted mightily to question Lewis about what he'd just said. Kate had not told him she'd said anything to old Jethro about what was between them. Then he remembered something; she'd started to tell him something down there before Lewis had shot her. Perhaps that was it.

'Well; maybe that took the fight out of old Jethro but by God it didn't bother me. As for shootin' her . . .'

Buck raised up slightly and called King Lewis the worst name he could lay tongue to.

Lewis stopped speaking at once. That wire-tight silence settled again. Buck looked swiftly around; Lewis was coming for him now. Only one of them would walk away from this near meeting.

The hush deepened; it drew out to its very limit. Buck waited and Lewis made no more sounds as he craftily went towards the place where Buck had been when he called Lewis that name. Minutes passed on leaden feet. Buck drew sideways a little so as to be protected from the rear. He pressed flat against stone there and shook sweat off.

Now there was no sound to place JG's rangeboss by. Buck thought Lewis must be crawling on all fours towards him through the rocks, otherwise he'd have heard that same sound of boots in the rocks. He looked quickly around; Lewis would have the area where Buck lay pinpointed by their talk, he had to move, to get farther north so that when they met Buck would be above Lewis and perhaps a little behind him.

There was a little gravelly passageway through rocks which appeared to angle north-westerly. He settled for that, twisted around and began inching his way along it. Several times he had to halt, carefully lift small rocks out of his way, place them silently aside, then crawl on. In this manner he managed to get a hundred feet beyond the place where he had been lying. Once, when he paused to listen, he thought he heard the sharp call of two men somewhere in the distance. These outcries came and they went, silence returned and he was not at all sure those haunting sounds hadn't been in his imagination.

Ultimately coming to a mighty, squatting boulder, which barred his path, Buck swung

168

right and left seeking another route. But the rimrocks this far northward were thicker than ever; no passageways showed among them and the only alternative to remaining where he was, lay in rising up and crawling over the stones to get behind that large boulder.

By now he was certain King Lewis would be close to that yonder place where he had been; perhaps lying just across the rocks from it. If he rose up now, if he made any sound or movement, he was sure JG's rangeboss would spy him. He turned, finally, put his back to the mighty boulder, looked back the way he had come and waited, blocking in all the onward area for some sign of his enemy.

Heat shimmered off that boulder at his back; it burnt against him from the overhead sky and it came up to singe through his clothing off the gritty earth. The yellow-hazed sun seemed not to have moved at all; it hung up there twice its normal size pouring cauldron-heat in a bitter blaze over everything.

Because the silence was complete, when a stone landed where Buck had been, back a hundred feet, it sounded extraordinarily loud. Another stone sailed over the rocks and struck against a granite slab, rattled down and fell into rank dust.

Buck swung his slitted eyes in the direction from which the stones were coming. He paid no attention to where they were landing. In this way he saw the third rock shoot up, make its high arc, and fall. Where that stone had begun its orbit was a large boulder with rusty lichen upon its north surface. Buck lifted his hand-gun, rested it upon a stone pile close at hand, steadied it there and waited.

Those stones stopped coming. Evidently Lewis was satisfied he was not going to make Buck reveal himself by this threadbare ruse. Time ran on again, hot and sticky and perilously silent. It was now a stalemate. Buck knew this and King Lewis also knew it, for he suddenly sprang up from behind that shielding big boulder, leapt wildly towards the place where Buck had been—and never once swung his head away from that spot to catch sight of Buck, a hundred feet off, also coming up into plain sight.

Lewis jerked from boulder to boulder. He stopped, sharply silhouetted against the brassy, pale sky, teetering upon the last row of rocks directly above the place where Buck had been. His Winchester, held low in both hands, was cocked and swinging.

Buck fired.

King Lewis, spring-tight, unwound in a mighty bound. That bullet had struck him somewhere in the body. He went drunkenly over the rocks into that little niche where Buck had been, whipped around in the direction of Buck's shot, and a totally unexpected thing happened. Three gunshots ripped out as one; except that Buck's six-gun, with its louder, deeper roar, was easily distinguishable over the sound of those other two weapons, which obviously were Winchester saddle-guns, those three shots blended so perfectly a distant listener could not have determined they were not just one weapon being fired.

King Lewis, caught flush by three bullets, was jerked around by them, impelled drunkenly along for some eight or ten feet, then dropped his own gun and collapsed across a pointed boulder. He hung there, arms lifelessly swinging, for a moment, slid off and crumpled in a ragged heap, face down in the stones.

Buck, more startled by those other Winchester shots than by Lewis's demise, ducked back out of sight. Evidently the other two men who had also shot Lewis had done the same thing, for as long as those diminishing echoes chased each other out over the far-away valley below, no one moved at all anywhere among the rimrocks.

'Hey, Buck,' a voice ultimately bellowed from southward. 'Hey, Buck; you all right?'

'I'm all right, yes. Who is that?' Buck yelled back.

'Me—Smith,' came his answer. 'I'll stand up. Now hold your fire, dammit.'

By removing his hat, placing his head low among the other head-shaped round boulders, Buck was able to peer ahead. He saw Smith come gingerly up to his feet, stand a moment in a half-crouch, then gradually straighten up entirely, shield his eyes and look ahead past King Lewis.

Buck let off a long sigh, brought up both arms, pushed against flinty soil and heaved himself upright for Smith to also see and recognise. The two of them started forward.

Now a third man rose up too. He was a little to one side of Smith. At sight of this man Buck stopped and stared. It was Hoyt McElroy. Hoyt said nothing but he broadly grinned. His teeth shone unnaturally white in the mahogany of his sun-layered dark face. He hefted a carbine and walked ahead, picking his way among the stones.

The three of them came together above the loose, flat body of King Lewis. Smith said, 'He never knew what hit him. All the same I'd have liked to seen his damned face just before he went down.' Smith looked away from Lewis; he ran a hard glance over Buck. Then his tough features broke into a wrinkly grin as Buck and Hoyt reached each other, threw out two big hands and violently shook.

Hoyt, in his dry-quiet way, said with a head-wag, 'It's got so's a feller can't leave you alone a few days you don't go climbin' mountains an' shootin' folks.' Hoyt nodded towards Lewis. 'Smith told me who this feller was.'

'I heard you two call out,' said Buck. 'It sounded like you were down on the pack-trail.'

'We werc,' said Hoyt McElroy. 'We were. I

172

got back a few minutes after you rode out of camp. I thought I'd find you at the herd, so I went out there. I come on to Smith here, and since I'd never seen him before I rode over an' we got to talkin'. He was tellin' me everything that's happened since I left, when we heard a gunshot up this here sidehill. We dusted it over here to investigate. We found the Graeme girl down there with a bandage on her head. I recognised that bandage, told Smith it was your neckerchief, an' about that time we heard another shot up here along this rim.' McElroy shrugged, looked away from the dead rangeboss, ran a critical look over Buck's torn and filthy clothing, said, 'Man; you're a mess. Let's get down from here.'

Smith held out his Winchester to Buck. 'Yours,' he said. 'I took it from your saddle-boot down where Miss Kate's lyin'.' His eyes were ironic. 'You don't want me packin' a gun, so take it.'

Buck pushed the gun back. 'Keep it,' he said, looking warmly at Smith. 'It's a present from me to you. I've got a nice-balanced extra six-gun at the wagons; that's yours too, when we get back.'

Hoyt was standing upon the lip of stone above the valley looking downward with a powerful scowl. 'We got to go back down there the same way we come up?' he asked the others. Buck and Smith said nothing, they just turned to look at Hoyt, who endured this stare for a moment, then shrugged, lost his frown and said, 'Well; I never did like heights, but then, since I figure this is as close to heaven as I'm likely to ever get, I might as well have a go at it.'

Hoyt got down gingerly, let himself down and began the perilous descent to the trail below. Smith followed him. Buck came last.

CHAPTER SEVENTEEN

The last man down the mountainside was Buck. Smith and Hoyt McElroy were already kneeling in the shimmering shade beside Kate Graeme. Smith, who appeared to have some knowledge of such injuries, closely examined the girl's wound, then said to Buck as he came up, 'We got to get her down out of here an' back to the river—somewhere close to water so we can keep wet cloths on her head an' face.' He stood up. 'I'll go back, get some of the boys, fetch back blankets and we'll make a stretcher to carry her on. You two fetch her down off this damned trail. We'll meet you at the bottom.' He looked from Buck to McElroy. 'All right?'

Buck said, 'Go ahead,' and dropped down beside Kate. She was still unconscious. Hoyt, gazing at the blood-matted hair, said with a low growl, 'That Lewis feller up there died too easy. What kind of a man would do a thing like this?'

Down-trail they heard Smith's horse kicking loose rocks into rattling cascades as the big man hurried recklessly back down to the valley below. Buck squatted there gazing upon Kate Graeme's white, composed face.

'Hoyt; I'm going to marry her.'

McElroy's head jerked around. He stared. 'She's right handsome all right,' he said. 'Pretty as any female I've ever seen, for a fact. But if what just half of what Smith's been tellin' me is true, Buck, her pappy's goin' to kill you if he can.'

'She had no hand in that, Hoyt.'

'No. No; from the looks of her I'd say she wouldn't have. But on the other hand . . .'

'Did you get the legal papers?' asked Buck, cutting across Hoyt's words.

McElroy nodded, slowly closing his lips, slowly putting his solemn gaze back upon Kate and offering to say nothing more.

'Then let's get down out of here with her.'

Hoyt didn't immediately move to obey this suggestion; for a little longer he hunkered there staring at Kate. Finally he got upright with a sigh, gravely shook his head, then moved over to assist Buck in stripping saddle-blankets from their mounts to fashion a sling for the unconscious girl.

Afterwards, when they had Kate balanced between them upon the improvised stretcher

175

and were stepping carefully down the trail, Hoyt said, 'Well; I'll tell you one thing. I don't know this lady at all, but danged if she's not solid as a rock. Must weigh close to a hundred and twenty pounds.' Hoyt went along with perspiration running freely over him from the load they carried.

It required a full hour for them to get down to the valley floor. There, Smith was waiting. He had Burton Riddle and six other men with him. Someone among them with experience or ingenuity or both, had tied a very professional horse-litter between two animals. Kate was gently placed upon this and the entire cavalcade started along northward towards the pothook wagon-camp. In order to protect their unconscious charge as much as possible these rough men, with a gentleness and thoughtfulness they did not appear upon the surface to have, took the long way to camp by keeping close to the river where tree-shade and cool river-air lessened the burning heat.

A cowboy went back after their horses. Another rider hurried ahead at Burton Riddle's command, to get several buckets of cold water from the river and fetch them to camp. Smith rode along beside Buck and Hoyt, who were on foot, watching the horses on either side of Kate with a careful eye.

They got to camp, made up a pallet beneath Riddle's texas, tenderly put Kate down there, and stepped aside as burly Buff Evans knelt beside the girl with an armload of clean rags which he dipped into those buckets of water, wrung out, and gently applied to Kate's cheeks and forehead.

The men stood helplessly watching. Several riders drifted in from the herd, other riders replaced them and rode out. The afternoon waned in its cooling way, shadows came creeping and that rusty-red pre-dusk light flamed out over the sky in long, coloured streamers.

Fred Naylor and Curt Walker came loping in side by side shortly ahead of the entire pothook crew. It was near supper time; Burt was busy at his chuck-box. Buck and Hoyt McElroy were a little apart from the others gravely talking. Laramie Potter and Percy Devlin were out with the horses.

A hundred feet from camp Walker bellowed out: 'Hey, ahead there! Big bunch of riders comin' from the south pass!'

If Walker had fired a shotgun through camp it could have produced no more instantaneous activity. Potter let out a savage growl and ran for his Winchester. Perc Devlin did the same. Every man except Buff Evans, Kate's self-appointed nurse, dropped whatever he was doing and ran grimly for weapons. Out where Hoyt and Buck were sitting together. McElroy's head lifted, his squinted eyes widened, and he said to Buck without looking away from all the fierce movement: 'What in the hell's got into them?'

Buck stood up, dusted his trousers and said, 'Kate. I know exactly how they feel.'

'Aw,' mumbled Hoyt, also rising up, 'that old man wouldn't send Lewis to shoot his own daughter, Buck. You know that.'

Buck said, 'I know it, but *they* don't. Come on. If it's sure-enough Graeme coming we'd better be out front or those boys'll never give him a chance to open his mouth. They're fightin' mad.'

The two pothook owners cut forward with long strides. Buck, shooting a glance southward, saw the bobbing, black and bunched-up approaching horsemen. 'It's JG all right,' he said to Hoyt. They got over where every man in the wagon-camp was positioning himself among friends; every man was armed and ready to fight. Some even had their carbines cocked. They looked ugly.

The man called Smith shouldered through to halt in front of Buck and Hoyt. He dwarfed the riders around him. 'I sent for her paw,' he told Buck. 'As soon as I got back here after the rimrock-fight, I sent a man over to JG for her paw.'

Buck was surprised at this and showed it. Hoyt, not so astonished, said, 'That answers the question why he's here. You did just right, Smith.' Hoyt brushed against Buck saying, 'Come on; maybe you didn't tell him to do that but he did right anyway. Come on, dammit.'

Buck turned slowly. He was faintly scowling but he went out ahead of his men with Hoyt and halted there watching that body of riders sweep up. No one spoke. Spread out belligerently behind Hoyt and Buck were the armed and ready pothook men.

While they waited for Graeme to get within speaking range Hoyt said, 'Buck; let's make Smith *segundo*. We need a rangeboss; you and I aren't always handy an' he's sure got the good sense for it.'

Buck said nothing. He was not completely recovered from his annoyance over Smith taking upon himself the responsibility for Kate's welfare yet.

'How about it?' Hoyt said, persisting.

'I'll think about it.'

'Oh hell; he did right an' you know it. You're just not used to havin' a man around who takes responsibility is all. I say we make him pothook rangeboss.'

Buck, seeing Jethro Graeme clearly now, seeing how the older man's face was grey and anxious, said, 'All right, Hoyt. Smith's our *segundo*.'

Buff Evans came pushing forward. He had his six-gun in its hip-holster but he had no carbine. He only wasted a very brief glance at JG's riding crew, then he said earnestly to Buck: 'She's comin' around. Them cold compresses took out most o' the swellin' an' I closed the wound. She said she's got a

179

headache, but you couldn't expect not to—getting hit like she did. Buck; she wants to see you.'

Handley, torn between old Graeme, who was less than twenty feet ahead now, and his daughter back at the camp, said, 'Go on back to her, Buff. Lace some hot coffee with whisky and get it down her. Make her comfortable, I'll be along directly.' He then stepped around Evans to face Jethro Graeme, who was dismounting where his men had halted.

'Where is my daughter?' the old cowman demanded, striding forward with big steps.

Hoyt McElroy stepped in front of him. Hoyt had both thumbs hooked in his shell-belt. He had a deceptively mild expression on his face. Graeme came on, head down and shoulders swinging. Without a word of warning Hoyt brought up a gnarled fist in a blur of speed. The blow cracked like a pistol shot against Jethro Graeme's jaw. He went down as though struck full-on by a sledgehammer. Behind him those mounted men gasped. Behind Hoyt and Buck sixteen Winchesters came up and sixteen pothook riders cocked them. The JG riders froze; not a gun appeared anywhere among them.

Hoyt stepped over, caught Graeme roughly by the arm and hauled him up to his feet. Graeme's eyes were turning aimlessly; he staggered and put up an exploratory hand to his jaw. Buck came up close to him.

180

'That's enough,' he said to Hoyt.

McElroy shrugged. He still looked mild—everywhere but in his smoky eyes—they were villainous to see.

Graeme gradually recovered. He worked his jaw, looked owlishly at Buck and said, 'Why did he do that?'

'I reckon he did it because you used to have a man in your employ who'd shoot women.'

Hoyt nodded solemn agreement with this. 'An' if you want to find that Lewis feller,' he told the old cowman, 'he's up there in the easterly rimrocks shot all to hell.'

Graeme's eyes shifted. 'Dead?' he asked Hoyt incredulously.

'Dead.'

'And—Kate . . . ?'

Buck took Graeme by the arm. He started past with him but Hoyt stopped them with a growl. He fished inside his shirt-pocket, brought forth several folded papers, caught hold of one of Graeme's hands and slapped the papers into them.

'Read 'em,' Hoyt growled. 'When you get time, Mister Graeme—read 'em.'

Jethro looked blankly at the papers. 'What are they?'

'Well, sir,' said Hoyt, his voice turning sardonic. 'Those happen to be legal deeds, recorded and plumb proper, showing that the entire Devil's Punch Bowl belongs to Buck Handley and Hoyt McElroy. There's another paper there too; I got it from the U.S. Marshal at the capital, Mister Graeme. It says "To Whom It May Concern", and then it says anyone trespassin' on Handley-McElroy land is liable to prosecution. It also says we got legal right to protect our land any way we have to.' Hoyt gave Graeme a rough push. 'Take him along,' he said to Buck. 'My fist's itchin' to bust him another one.'

Graeme, still gripping those papers in his fist, passed through the unsmiling file of pothook riders with Buck steering him.

Kate was sitting up when Buck and her father walked over to her. She smiled at them but Buff Evans, there on his knees beside her, gave Jethro Graeme a venomous look.

Buck dropped down beside the girl opposite her father. She took his hand, squeezed it hard, turned to look at her father and say: 'I told you I loved him. Now I can also tell you that he loves me . . . Father . . . ?'

Old Jethro worked his jaw a little, gingerly. He didn't say anything for a moment but his face softened from its habitual hardness and his gaze passed above his daughter to consider Buck.

'All right, Kate,' he said, still looking straight at Buck. 'He wins. The two of you win.'

Jethro pushed out a big scarred hand. Buck met it half way. Those two iron-like men shook and Kate put her right hand gently over their gripping fists. There was a scald of tears in her

We hope you have enjoyed this Large Print book. Other Chivers Press or Thorndike Press Large Print books are available at your library or directly from the publishers.

For more information about current and forthcoming titles, please call or write, without obligation, to:

Chivers Press Limited
Windsor Bridge Road
Bath BA2 3AX
England
Tel. (01225) 335336

OR

G.K. Hall & Co.
295 Kennedy Memorial Drive
Waterville
Maine 04901
USA

All our Large Print titles are designed for easy reading, and all our books are made to last.